BENOIT

Owatonna U Hockey, 3

RJ SCOTT
V.L. LOCEY

Love Lane Books

Benoit, Owatonna U Hockey, 3

Copyright © 2019 RJ Scott, Copyright © 2019 V.L. Locey

Cover design by Meredith Russell, Edited by Sue Laybourn

Published by Love Lane Books Limited

ISBN: 9781785645525

All Rights Reserved

Dedication

To my family who accepts me and all my foibles and quirks. Even the plastic banana in my holster.
VL Locey

Always for my family,
RJ Scott

BENOIT

OWATONNA U HOCKEY#3

RJ SCOTT &
V.L. LOCEY

Love Lane Books

ONE

Benoit

MOVE-IN DAY.

Senior year.

Final season with the Eagles.

Last chance to be the breakout young goalie that Edmonton would *not* pass up for a future higher draft pick.

No pressure.

"Mom, where are the water bottles?" I shouted from my new room on the second floor of the house Ryker and Scott had insisted I move into. The house Ryker's father had bought and Scott and Hayne called home, although they lived in the attic/studio.

Chucking clothes aside, I then dug into bag after bag, looking for the small plastic bottles of fresh, clear Canadian water we'd packed. "Oh no, come on." I whipped a sneaker over my head. Why had I packed one Nike but not the other? "Where are they?"

"Dude, seriously, I nearly suffered blunt head trauma walking past your door," Ryker said, flinging the blue Nike back into my room.

I spun, my hands in fists, and gaped at my friend, and now fellow housemate, staring at me. "I can't find the water. Ryker, I'm seriously freaking out. You know this American water isn't fit for my crease. Have you seen my water? Where's my mother?"

"Ben, breathe. Do the yoga stuff. In. Out. In. Out." He padded into my room, hands up in a placating manner, his eyes nearly obscured by long wavy hair. Hair he'd let grow out over the summer for Jacob, his boyfriend, who was now back on the farm, several hours away from campus.

"Right, yeah, calming breaths. I'm okay now." I sat on the edge of my bed, closed my eyes, and focused on inhaling and exhaling. Ryker dropped down beside me, looping an arm around my shoulders. "It's cool. No worries. If I forgot them, Mom will just ship me more."

"Totally correct," Ryker said, leaning into my side a bit. "Your mom is on top of things. And your sister…"

"Dude, don't talk about my sister unless it's to say she's amazing, because she is."

"I wasn't going to say anything about Tamara other than she's super amazing."

Right. I knew guys. I was one. I might not have been straight or even bi, I tended to think of myself as pan or omni, if picking categories was essential, which it's not, but society gets hung up on labels. I tended to fall for people first and not worry over genders. Heart matters, not genitals. I did kind of dig older men for some reason, but other than that, I was open to dating anyone.

"And is really pretty."

I opened my eyes, turned my head, and gave Ryker my best touch-her-and-die big brother look.

"And is only seventeen," I reminded him. "And why are you checking out my sister when you have a boyfriend?"

"What? Am I dead or something? Jacob and I are allowed to look, discreetly. Man, why did you mention him?" He groaned, falling back onto my naked mattress as if he'd been shot with a crossbow. "It was like five whole minutes since I last thought of him. Seriously, Ben, I think I'm going to fucking die without him here this year."

"Nah, you'll be good. You can visit on weekends." I patted his thigh.

"Sure, when the roads are passable, which is hardly ever in the winter. You're smart. You've totally avoided the agony of relationships and focused on hockey. Dad told me to do that but then... Jacob." He sighed dramatically. "I'm going to die. I can feel it. Death is imminent."

I wanted to say something but bit down on any reply. Honestly, it wasn't that I didn't want someone in my life; I did. It was an aching hole inside me. Being the fifth wheel *all the time* sucked. But I hadn't found the right person, and this year dating was taking a massive backseat to hockey and studying. I *had* to maintain good grades, and I *had* to make sure Edmonton didn't let me slip through their fingers. They had thirty days after I graduated. If they opted out? Well, they just couldn't opt out. I'd dreamed of playing for them ever since I was old enough to stand on skates. I'd grown up idolizing Grant Fuhr and then had added Malcolm Subban to my list of black goalies to emulate if and when I had the chance to go pro. I *had* to make it. For my heroes, for my family, and for myself and all the black kids who wanted to play the game.

No pressure at all.

"Looking for these, maybe?" Tamara asked, stepping into the doorway, in jean shorts and a flowery little summer top, holding my precious bottles of Quebec water. "He okay?"

"Yeah, he's mourning his boyfriend." I shot up, leaving Ryker spread out on my bed making odd, pained noises.

"Oh my God, is he dead?" my sister, who really *is* the prettiest and sweetest thing ever, gasped.

"No, just graduated," I explained, taking the four half-gallon containers and hugging them to my chest. People might think that importing water from your home lake was stupid, but it wasn't. American water wasn't pure enough. It made the ice bumpy. I know. I'm a goalie. I have a relationship with the ice in my crease. Some tendies talk to their pipes. I groomed my ice with tender loving care, and it loved me in return. Maybe I should start dating my ice…

"I see she found you," Mom said, carrying my pads into the room, Jared Madsen on her heels, with another box full of skates and several goalie sticks under his arms. He seemed as tired as my mother did. Kind of worried too. Guess he was more concerned about Ryker than he let on, although I'd known he was worried when he'd called me at home in Stanstead over the summer to ask me to move in here with Ryker to keep him company and on track. I'd promised I'd do my best, but it was asking a lot.

"Yeah, thanks." I hurried to relieve my mom of my gear. Mr. Madsen dumped his armful onto the bed, covering Ryker, who lay there whining softly.

"Ryker, you have a ton of stuff yet to move in. Come on." Mr. Madsen patted Ryker's denim-covered knee, gave me a weak smile, and then left us to it.

Ryker sat up, blinked, and slouched off to help his dad with his boxes and bags. Tamara began decorating, looking for a box of thumbtacks and getting my posters of Malcolm in net and Swollen Members unrolled. Every time Mom looked at the rap group from Vancouver, she would roll her eyes at their name. Mom and Dad were more Smokey Robinson or Teddy Pendergrass lovers, although Mom had said that if she were thirty years younger, Drake would be in trouble.

"You look tense. Why are you tense already? School or hockey hasn't even started," Mom asked a few minutes later while we were making my bed. A double. No way did a twin fit me anymore. She shook out the flat sheet, and it drifted down over the fitted sheet hugging the mattress. "Honey, you have to remember what your father told you. The weight of the world does not rest on your shoulders. Nor does our situation."

"I know," I replied while I shoved the ends of the sheet under the mattress.

I heard her tut and glanced from the wadded-up sheet to her proud face. Tiny but strong, Mom had been carrying the brunt of the financial situation at home since my father had been diagnosed with sarcoidosis, an inflammatory disease that affects his organs. It was a condition that none of us had ever heard of before. Abnormal masses grow in the affected organs. For my father, it was his lungs and lymph nodes. His had gone undiagnosed for a long time, his persistent cough related to his damn smoking habit, or so we'd all assumed. His condition was chronic, and his lungs and vision were already compromised. Things had changed so much in one summer.

One day he'd gone in for a physical when he'd

changed jobs and—*BAM*—the chest X-ray had shown some suspicious spots. It had been really stressful finding the right team of doctors and the correct diagnosis. Thank God we lived in Canada. The medical bills for his treatment and doctors would have bankrupted us if we'd lived here in the States.

Dad now suffered from shortness of breath, fatigue, and swollen joints, which kept him at home for the most part and unable to work. That was where he was now, home, running a course of meds while resting and grumbling about being on oxygen at fifty. Not being able to drive me to campus also upset him. As did the possibility of missing my games. He was my biggest fan.

If I could make a splash this season, the scouts would be all over me, talking me up, and I'd hopefully get an invite to a rookie tournament and maybe training camp. If I worked hard, I might make the team. Then I'd be making money. *Real* money. Money that would help ease the burden of my dad's illness and the cost of my college education, as well as Tamara's. This year was beyond important. There could be no distractions.

"You know, but you're not taking it to heart," Mom replied, as she always did whenever we discussed life and Dad's illness.

Tamara leaped into the conversation, my favorite poster of Drake in her hand. "Okay, so how about we put Drake over the bed? This way you look up at him at night while you—"

"*Tamara*!" Mom gasped, erasing the creeping unease that was settling on the room.

"What? I was going to say he could look at him at

night while he tries to fall asleep. God, Mom, you're such a pervert."

I chuckled at my sister. Always keenly aware of tension and doing her best to alleviate it. The rest of the afternoon passed quickly, and before I was ready, I was hugging my mother and sister goodbye out in the street. Mr. Madsen had left as well.

"Tell Dad I love him." I held the passenger side door open for my mother. Tamara was driving back home. Poor Mom. I'd ridden with my sister in the past. She tended to lose track of things like speed limits when she was bopping around to whatever K-Pop band the girls were obsessing over at the moment. Not that I blamed her for her love of Asian men, but safety first, seriously.

"I want you to promise me that you'll take time for things besides hockey." Mom took my chin in her hand, forcing me to stare into big brown eyes just like mine and Tamara's.

"She means find a boyfriend," Tamara tossed out as she buckled in. "Or a girlfriend. Just get out of your head and enjoy senior year."

I was going to reply, but the K-Pop flared to life. Mom rolled her eyes, kissed me on the cheek, and then released my chin. I closed the door soundly, patted the roof, and hurried to get back onto the curb before Tamara ran over my toes.

Poor Mom. I wasn't sure I could do over twenty hours of BTS no matter how mouthwatering Asian guys were. Good thing they had a hotel lined up for the night. Mom would need the break. They pulled away, I waved, and then Scott appeared at my side, his thick arm resting around my neck.

"We're doing stir-fry for dinner. You want some?"

I nodded, gave the taillights of my mother's car a long last look, and then ambled back into the house, the smell of the fresh paint on the walls still strong. Ryker's dads—dad and stepdad, but Tennant had informed us that we must call him "Ryker's Pop" just to twist Ryker's nuts—had dropped some big cash into the place. New paint, carpeting, and a whole house rewire to get things up to code. It was nice now, clean and tidy, which I preferred. My old place had been a pigsty, and no matter how much Jacob and I had pleaded with the other guys on the team, they just would not pick up after themselves.

In the small kitchen, Hayne threw us a glance over a bare shoulder, his smile timid but welcoming. He had blue paint on his nose and in his wild curls. The guy was totally cute, shy around us yet, but not as bad as he had been, and madly in love with Scott. They kissed all the time. We sat down at the secondhand table and ate, the four of us, talking about our final year at OU while forking in pork, green peppers, mushrooms, bok choy, and broccoli florets. Hayne had graduated last year and was trying to make a go of it as an artist. The meal was perfect for athletes. I scraped the last spoonful of food out of the wok, playfully tussling over it with Ryker until Scott stole the plate from my hand and wolfed down the remains in one massive inhalation.

"Dude!" Ryker shouted, threw an arm around Scott's neck, and they rolled to the floor, wrestling and laughing. I jumped back, as did Hayne, both of us leaping up to sit on the counters until a victor was decided.

"Who do you pick to win?" I asked Hayne.

"Mm, maybe Scott."

"Okay, I'll take Ryker to win. Loser cleans the kitchen."

Hayne nodded, curls falling into his face, and we shook. Five minutes later, I was elbow deep in soap bubbles since the dishwasher was still waiting for the repairman to arrive.

"Dude cheats," Ryker grumbled. "Tickling is totally not a wrestling move."

"Just dry faster, giggle goose."

"'Giggle goose'? Really?"

"Just dry."

"Canadians are lame chirpers."

The second wrestling match of the night ended with Ryker washing *and* drying. Someone had to represent Canada and our chirping ability. Sitting on Ryker's back while shoving my wet fingers into his ears had taught him a lesson he'd not soon forget. Truthfully, we'd both laughed like fools throughout the wet willy episode. It was kind of hard to stay mad at Ryker.

After dinner, I took a walk around campus, skates slung over my shoulder. Kids were rolling in from all over the country, and Canada, of course. The hockey and football programs here were top-notch. Stopping along the way to the rink, small squirt bottle in my back pocket, I chatted with a few returning students, several inviting me and the guys—Ryker and Scott—to this party or that party. People always wanted jocks at their parties. I smiled politely because I *am* Canadian and said we'd see if we could make it.

I had no intention of going to any parties this year

unless they were team-sponsored events. Ryker going was doubtful, not without Jacob at his side, and Scott needed to stay as far away from booze and dope as he could get. Plus, Scott was happy at home with Hayne, cuddling on the couch, kissing and touching, whispering as lovers do. A twang of envy flared to life as I strolled around the quad. I swallowed that down like a sour belch. There was no point in dwelling over romance. This year I was a monk. Just call me Father Morin. No parties, no sex, no falling in love with this girl's eyes or that guy's lips. Work, study, focus, serenity. Those were *my* four agreements, my personal guide to making sure life went as I needed it to go.

Passing the massive football stadium, skates draped casually over my shoulder, I slipped into the hockey rink, the warm August air replaced by the snap of artificial cold. I breathed in the smell of ice and men and felt a knot in my shoulders loosen. It had always been this way with me and hockey. The sounds, the smells, the speed, and the competition. It was close to a religious experience or perhaps even a sexual one.

"Brain, you've *got* to stop with the sex shit, okay? We're chaste this year, remember?" I mumbled, trotting along toward the Eagles locker room, then hanging a right to the tunnel that led to the ice. And there it was. Eagles home ice. The screaming raptor already painted into the circle at the center ice. The ice was pristine, untouched by any skate, virginal, innocent of the way of barbaric hockey players who would gouge it up and spit on it, bleed and fight on it, strive to make dreams come true on it. It was chaste, and I was going to pop its... "Brain, come on, we've got to stop this. Trust me, it's going to be a *long* dry spell. We need to focus on the important things."

I needed to go home and meditate. But this took precedence. I sat on the Eagles bench, toed off my ratty sneakers, and slid my feet into my goalie skates. The ice glittered and winked at me, an alluring temptation. The only temptation that I could indulge in for two semesters.

When blade touched ice, the tension centered in my chest eased. I skated to my crease, the blue in front of the net unspoiled. I dropped to one knee, ran my hand over it, felt the cold seep into my fingertips, and closed my eyes.

"I'll treat you well, pretty ice. Make you stronger, but in return, I ask you to take care of me as I care for you." My pathetic poem to the ice had been the same since I was ten. I lifted my fingers to my lips, kissed them, and then placed the kiss to the ice. The hum of the air-conditioners and two men working floated over me. "Know that when I do this, I'm working to make us both more powerful."

I stood up, pulled out my small bottle of water from Quebec, and squirted it over the blue. Then, with a soft apology, I began working the ice, using my blades to chew it up into fine powder, mixing the better ice—from my home lake—into the Minnesota ice. I scraped and I patted until I felt it was perfect. Then I turned to caress the pipes, which I felt lacked the magic of ice but were still my friends. The pipes were like Ryker, a buddy, but the ice was like a lover and required tenderness.

When I was done, I stood off to the side of my net, admiring the marriage of American and Canadian ice, then went off to find the Zamboni driver to let him know that my crease was not to be touched by him or his machine until after our first team practice. He nodded but looked at me as if I'd lost my marbles. Whatever. Only another goalie would understand. That ice was now mine, and I'd protect it passionately, just as I would a sweetheart. I'd caress it and coo to it, stroke it until it trembled with need and begged me to…

"Right, off to meditate."

TWO

Ethan

"OH WOW, MR. GIRARD, IT'S YOUR BIRTHDAY," PERKY-nurse Two said with a smile.

"Yep, it is." I'd been in the hospital an hour, and in that time I'd been reliably informed it was my birthday on six separate occasions. I'd actually run out of ways to say that yes, it was my birthday, yes, it was a shame I'd broken a leg on said birthday, and no, I didn't have anything planned for when I got out of the hospital. So now, I was just sticking to a simple *yep* because I was tired, grumpy, and never thought I'd turn thirty-two stuck in a bed in the emergency room of Owatonna Hospital.

"Not a good place to spend the day," she added.

"You're telling me," I said and rolled my eyes theatrically before staring back at my leg in an effort to discourage more talking. The last nurse had remonstrated at length about how if only Boston had tightened their D-Corp in game four… blah, blah. I'd heard it all before, and I didn't want to hear it again.

"I'm here to take blood." She pulled a cloth from a

container, and I knew it held needles and vials, but I sure as hell wasn't looking. I'm a defenseman in the freaking NHL. I can get hit by a puck, have a tooth hanging by a thread that I'll yank out, and still go back out on next shift. I work through pain. I deal with blood. That is who I am. But needles freak me the hell out.

"You'll feel a pinch," she advised.

"Just a small prick," I offered because that was my default when I was anxious; I joked, messed around, got very unserious. "Said the intern to the President," I added and made myself smile. If I can't be amused at my own stupid jokes, then who can?

"There, all done."

And now I waited for the next part. Most of the staff I'd seen, medical and admin, had known who I was. Living in Minnesota equaled hockey in the blood, but playing for Boston meant, in most Owatonna residents' eyes, I was playing for the wrong team. The admin assistant who'd booked me in politely informed me, in a very nice way, that Boston sucked, I sucked, and worse of all, Brady Rowe sucked.

Of course, she also asked what it was like playing with *that sexy* Brady Rowe, and did I know his brother Tennant Rowe, and wasn't Ten cute? I was used to it.

My doctor, whose name was Doctor De'ath, I kid you not, joked that he'd sell the news of my lower body injury to the Minnesota team. I had to point out it was unlikely he'd make any money from news about a lowly third line D-Man. I'd been flippant with him, but there was truth in every word.

Me aged eighteen seemed a long time ago, but having been drafted at that age directly into the Boston farm program, working my way into the NHL team, I'd never known anything but hockey. Now fourteen years later, thirty-two was past it, old, over the hill, tired, and worst of all I was a player without a contract.

Which is why I'd run the car into a post.

Not deliberately, of course. My agent, Eli Craven, had informed me that a possible contract might not be happening, maybe, and that I'd find myself on the open market. There were so many translations of the word *possible* in that sentence that it was obvious he was telling me I was done with Boston.

He didn't have to tell me; I kind of knew. Fourteen years, and I was finding it harder and harder to keep up with the young guys. Not to the point where I couldn't do my job; I was still one of the top fifty D-Men in the NHL or at least top seventy-five. But just enough so that my bones ached, and I was exhausted, particularly as Boston had made it to the third round of the playoffs, which meant a longer playing season.

But yeah, I'd been listening to Eli telling me all of this news about my contracts, on speakerphone in my sleek and sexy Maserati, and I'd pulled off the highway in order to hear him better. I'd taken a parking space outside Aldi, not realizing it wasn't a space at all and that a post was right *there*. Unfortunately, I didn't break my leg by hitting the post. At least if I had done, then I could exaggerate, call it injury after a car accident. But it wasn't the smash that had taken me down and fractured my leg.

No, that was me falling up a curb *after* the accident. Maybe I'd been shaken, possibly I hadn't seen the height of the curb, or it could have been that my right knee gave way as it sometimes did.

Whatever it was, I'd face-planted in front of a group of concerned moms pushing carts and with my leg twisted in that freak way that had never happened to me on ice.

"Ethan, what the fuck did you do to your car?"

Great, who called Robbie? The last thing I needed was my little brother up in my face and causing chaos. That was another problem with sitting here in the same hospital I'd been born in, for God's sake. News of me being in here would eventually have reached my family. An hour—that was all it had taken.

"Who told you I was here?" I grumped, the pain meds not quite taking the edge off the constant throb of pain.

He counted off on his fingers. "Chief told me that Sevvy called him to say that Amber called him to say you were carted off in an ambo, and to tell me that Yan and Iris saw your car, and that you'd totaled it."

I closed my eyes. "I didn't total my car."

"Amber told Sevvy that Iris said it looked totaled to her."

"Iris is exaggerating. I scraped a bumper on a post, is all."

"Well, the chief said Sevvy heard the whole front was gone. Jeez, Ethan, I can't believe you broke your car," he said and sat heavily on the side of the bed, the whole mattress dipping and causing me to slide sideways, which *freaking hurt.*

"Get off me, you moron," I blurted, but he didn't budge. If anything, he bounced a little because Robbie Girard is a giant pain-in-the-ass brother who needs me to pummel him into the ground.

"What the hell is this?" He pointed at my beard, the wild bushy affair that I couldn't be bothered to tame.

"Well, you see, when a boy becomes a man, they can grow beards, and one day, Robbie, you'll be able to grow one too."

He bounced again. "You look like a fucking hippy."

"And you stink," I observed as the scent of smoke and grease overwhelmed me.

He sniffed himself and wiped a black smudge from his arm. "House fire on Third, cake pan. It's okay though. I heroically and single-handedly, extinguished the fire."

"Heroically my ass. I bet you were the one at the back holding a bucket."

He smoothed his hand down his T-shirt emblazoned with the logo of the Owatonna Fire Department and then kissed each of his flexed biceps.

"It's a big bucket," he announced, "and not to change the subject, but you'll be pleased to know Mom's on her way." He grinned at me so wide it must have hurt.

I fell back on the pillow and groaned. "Why?"

"Well, Sevvy and Amber called her. Then Iris and—"

"Yeah, yeah, I get it." I twisted my head to glance left at the chair next to the bed where my cut-up jeans and scuffed boots sat. I'd skated with worse than a fractured leg. Maybe I should just get my stuff and leave before Momma Girard descended on the hospital, with my poor dad in tow.

"I was just the first Girard to get here," Robbie said, and distracted by checking out a passing nurse, he shifted forward on the bed, which made the mattress move again.

"Jesus, asshole, get off my bed."

He smirked at me because that was what brothers did to each other, and then he grew more serious and pulled the chair over to the side of the bed, shoving my possessions to the floor before settling in for the long haul.

"Seriously though, Eeth, are you okay?"

I narrowed my eyes at him; we messed around, we wound each other up, we fought and sniped and loved each other unconditionally, but Robbie being sincere was a red flag.

"Why?" I asked.

He leaned forward and took my hand, held it tight. "As your only sibling, if you die, can I have your car?"

I shook off his hold and punched at him, missing, rolling, and catching my damn leg, pain radiating up to my thigh.

"Wait until I can goddamn walk," I breathed through the worst of it. He was just far enough away to know that I couldn't reach him, sitting there grinning at me.

Two could play at that game. "How's Gabby?" I asked the question as if I didn't know for absolutely sure that our childhood neighbor Gabby, the focus of Robbie's unrequited love, had moved out of town two months back.

Robbie grabbed at his chest. "That's low," he muttered, "but she texted me." He pulled out his cell phone, scrolling through his messages and then thrusting the phone under my nose. "See, what do you think that means?"

I read the text and nodded. "She misses you," I announced.

He appeared hopeful, and for a moment I felt sorry for him. Then I recalled that there was no room for pity in sibling get-back.

"You think?" he asked with optimism.

"Nothing says a girl is missing you like texting you a

picture of her eating a hot dog in New York," I summed up and couldn't help the laugh tweaking at my lips. I desperately tried to hold it in, but it came out as a sudden snort.

Indignant, he pocketed the cell. "I don't care what you think. I take it that she's subliminally suggesting a blow job."

"Robert Justin Girard, what in the blazes are you talking about!" The voice was strident, and I sank into the bed at the same rate as Robbie subsided in his chair. He didn't look like a rough-and-tough firefighter now. If anything, he was just a little boy caught out by his mom.

"Hi, Mom," he offered weakly.

She cuffed him around the head, then hurried to my side, pressing a hand to my forehead as all the best moms do.

"You're not hot," she announced as she used to when we were kids attempting to get off school. "How are you feeling, sweetheart?"

"I'll be okay," I said with just the right amount of stoic bravery. I saw Robbie making gagging motions in my peripheral vision.

She picked up my notes and tutted. Never let it be said that Margaret Girard didn't try to understand everything that touched her kids, but I doubt the chart made any sense to her.

"Your dad was worried," she announced, and behind her, Dad sketched a wave.

"Hey, son."

"Hey, Dad."

That was my dad, a man of few words, mostly because he never got a word in edgeways.

"Where is Doctor De'ath?" Mom peered around us like a meerkat protecting us from eagles.

"He was called away on an emergency—"

"Doesn't he realize how much of an emergency this is? Does he not remember who you are?" she snapped. Cue Robbie with more gagging motions, and me sinking into the bed hoping it would swallow me whole. "This is your entire career on the line. Have you called the team? Can they not fly you to Boston? What about that nice Brady Rowe? He must have a jet by now, or he could pay for one. The team could as well. I only want the best for my son. And you need to shave your beard now. How will you train with all that hair, and will you be able to train with a broken leg?"

I was lost for words, and I didn't even try to form a coherent sentence in reply to anything she said, and *thank fuck* Dr. De'ath appeared behind them and threw me one of those looks, the kind I'd grown up seeing whenever my mom was around. She was notorious for not holding back, but she was also fiercely protective of her boys, and I'm sure Dr. De'ath was aware of just how bumpy things could get. He closed the door behind him and then slid past Mom, who shot him a glare that would have quelled a lesser man.

"Can we talk?" he asked and side-eyed my mom.

"It's okay. They can stay. Means I don't have to explain it all again later."

"Okay, well, I've looked at the X-rays," he placed them on the lightbox and stood back. "You have a clean break in the tibia, which is good news. You're not looking at surgery, in my opinion, just a cast, and then therapy, which I assume you'll be undertaking with the team. I can certainly talk to the team physician and send on X-rays to him."

"I guess," I said in my best noncommittal way, ignoring the narrow-eyed glare from Mom. "We can just do it all here if it's a simple break."

"What about medical concerns with the team?" Robbie asked, and I hated that the only time he was going to be serious was asking me leading questions. I ignored him.

Dr. De'ath interjected in his best diplomatic tone. "We'll get your brother sorted and on his way home."

That was somewhat of an issue. I didn't actually have my own place in Owatonna. After all, I was only supposed to be there for two weeks. After that, there was the Bahamas with Lester *Lemmy* LeMan, a fellow Boston D-Man, for fishing, diving, and food. Not to mention I needed to be in Boston with my agent and the team management, in case negotiations were required.

I was staying for the two weeks in the one-bedroom, half-bath extension over Mom and Dad's garage, much to Robbie's amusement, who never failed to comment on the millions he said I was hoarding. I missed my loft, with its feet of space, and the huge carved-oak bed, and the privacy, but the two weeks in the summer with my parents and idiot brother grounded me.

Could I last more than two weeks within spitting distance of Mom?

I need to rent a house. Stat.

The doctor was talking, and I was listening, at least I was trying. Mom was mumbling about experts, Dad was soothing her, and Robbie was tapping the arm of his chair to some unheard rhythm in his head.

"Guys, let's clear the room," Dr. De'ath announced, and thank fuck for small mercies, they left.

I love my family before even hockey, but sometimes…

"Wait, Robbie?" I called, and he turned to face me. I tossed him the keys to the Maserati. "She's outside the Aldi. Not a scratch, okay, and don't go over thirty."

He caught the keys with a wide grin and winked at me.

"I mean it, not a scratch."

He gave me the finger and smirked. "Says the man who nearly wrote the car off."

"I scraped a post!" Too late. He'd pulled the door shut behind him, and I shook my head, then turned my attention back to the doc who had cleared his throat pointedly.

"I'll type this up," he began. "Then I can talk to the team and forward the X-rays."

"It's okay. You don't need to." I leveled him with a look that I hoped conveyed that he didn't need to talk to the team. I don't know if he thought I was hiding this or if he could see the thoughts of retirement that sometimes sat in my head.

"Of course," he murmured.

"Thank you."

Retirement was an option. If I was done, if I didn't have a contract, was I willing to work hard on getting a contract in Europe? Or go down to AHL level? Shouldn't I quit while I was ahead: two championship rings, two-time winner of the Norris Trophy, and three times an All-Star? Retiring now meant I would go out on a high, and I could find something else to define my life. I had so much money I didn't know what to do with it, cars, my loft, vacations, but I was ready for something else.

And what will I do with my life now?

Fear gripped me as I lay there waiting for the nurse. What would I do? Coach maybe? TV commentator? Become an insurance salesman? Live off my millions and never work another day again? Take up veteran tenpin bowling?

I'm so scared.

THE HOUSE WAS EXTENSIVE, a huge warren of wide-open rooms, light spilling through skylights, a covered pool, a game room, a cinema room, and the rent wasn't much more than my loft had been in the city.

"I'll take it," I said, impulsively deciding this was exactly the place I needed to be right now. I crutched into the kitchen, resting against the counter, and marveled at the size of the fridge. An entire hockey team could fit in there.

"I do have other properties to show you," Sevvy said and placed details on the side. Sevvy was Robbie's best friend, and just like my brother, he hadn't quite gotten over the damage I'd done to my car. At least, he didn't keep stealing my keys and driving each and every firefighter at Station Six to the market and back, though. I needed to hide the damn keys. Only I wasn't really as bothered as I liked to make out. Robbie loved that damn car as if it was his, and I'd already decided he could have it. Cars like that need to be loved, and for me it was just a way of getting from A to B. I wanted to get something more practical, for when I was okay to drive.

"I don't need to see anywhere else. I like this place. Can you start the paperwork? When can I move in?"

"As you can see, it's empty, so it's available as soon as your check clears."

I hobbled to face him. "I'll transfer the cash. I want to move in today."

"Today?"

"Yep. I want to stay and not leave, right now."

"References—"

"Phone Boston. I'll give you a direct number, and they'll send you something now."

Just like that, I was renting a prime piece of real estate, thirty minutes from my parents, closer to the edge of town, and it was peaceful and huge. I called Robbie, asked him to bring my stuff over from Mom's, and told him that no, I wasn't worried that Mom might catch him and he should stop being such a kid.

By day three in my new place, I was totally chill, watching crap on Netflix, catching up on shows I thought I might like, and on day four, my agent phoned.

"I can't see you getting a contract with Boston. It's not your time right now, but I do have an offer from—"

"I'm retiring, Eli."

He sighed. "I thought you'd say that, and I might have some gigs as a commentator for you."

"Maybe. I don't know what I'm doing, or who I even am now. I'll call you when I know for sure. Is that okay?"

"Of course."

"And, Eli?"

"Yeah?"

"Thank you for fourteen years. I owe you so much."

"Awww, kid, I'm gonna miss your face."

By day six, I'd caught up on *Game of Thrones* and a show about tidying houses. I didn't really have anything to tidy in this house. I'd asked Lemmy to arrange someone to pack up and send on everything they could from the loft, and my former teammate assured me it would all arrive on the weekend. I spent a long time staring at my beard in the hallway mirror. It certainly meant that not many people would recognize me. Add a ball cap and I could be incognito. But the beard was a jungle, and I should do something about it.

"Another day."

By day seven, I was losing my shit, the walls closing in on me, so I called a cab with no idea of a destination until we drove past the Owatonna U. Campus.

And I knew exactly what I needed.

Ice.

Security let me through after I gave some autographs and listened to him talk about how sad it was I'd ended up in Boston and how he wished I'd played for Minnesota. I agreed with him, just for an easy life, even though the Boston team was my blood. Finally, I was able to crutch through the entrance to the ice and found a quiet space behind a screen. I inhaled the scent of the place and closed my eyes. The noise of a conversation as two men approached my small hiding space filled the silence.

"I have no idea. He poured water from a bottle right on the ice and then told me to leave it."

"That's the kid in goal, Ben-Lar or something French and fancy sounding."

"Yeah, well, I didn't touch it, but if someone goes all health and safety on me and warns me that…"

They passed me by unseen, and I let out a small breath. I kind of liked my quiet space and shifted a little to take the pressure off my right leg. I stayed there until a group of small kids swarmed onto the ice, and then I moved to sit in one of the seats and watched all the tiny future NHL'ers learn how to skate.

The scrape of blades on ice, shrieks, the noise of sticks and laughing?

This was home.

THREE

Benoit

KIDS ON ICE. THEY ALWAYS AMUSED ME AND SWARMED around me like little gnats, making all kinds of noise and asking a ton of questions. I did my best to hang out with them and pass along what knowledge I could. I liked kids, a lot. Which was why I was getting a degree in early childhood education. If and when hockey wasn't priority number one, I wanted to teach.

Sometimes, all it took was one encouraging word to get a child on the right track, to inspire, to guide. When I was seven, I'd had the privilege of meeting one of my idols at a signing at a local convention center after he'd retired. He'd not only signed my stick, but he'd told me he was proud of me and my dedication to the sport. That fat stick signed by Mr. Fuhr still hung on my bedroom wall back home. One person can make a huge difference in a kid's life. Someday, I hoped I could be the one to inspire.

After about thirty minutes, I had to hand things over to the peewee coach. With a wave, I skated to the Eagles bench, took my skates off, slid my sneakers back on, and jogged down the chute, past the locker and PT room, and headed to the main doors. Tomorrow was the first day, and I had a meeting with my advisor about some classes that I hadn't registered for but had been placed into anyway. We also had to talk about me being part of the pre-student teacher program. As I rounded the corner by the Eagles gear shop, I found some guy trying to open the door as he wobbled around on crutches. His language was colorful to say the least, especially when he lost his left crutch.

"Hey, sir! Sir, let me help you out here," I shouted, running up to him to place my hand on his arm. "Someday they'll have some handicap accessible doors installed here."

I smiled at him as he turned to check whoever was grabbing his arm. Our gazes touched, and I felt this spark ignite in my lower belly. He was incredibly hot, with blue eyes the same color as the lake back home. Beautiful azure eyes under well-formed eyebrows, one with a thin scar, thick dark lashes, and lips that seemed to curl up at the edges with ease. Older than me; that was obvious by the small lines around his eyes, laugh lines. Must be he smiled a lot. That was good. I liked men who smiled frequently. I even dug his beard, to a point. If it had been trimmed down close instead of wild and wooly, he'd have been all kinds of sinful. His eyes held my attention. They were familiar for some reason...

"'Sir,' huh?" he asked, his voice deep and dark, like the inside of a whiskey barrel. "That doesn't make me feel old or feeble or anything."

I bent down to grab his crutch, my eyes skating over him. Tall, lean, hard, thick thighs and meaty calves, or I guess I should say thigh and calf. One leg was all casted up, the plaster covered with signatures and lewd drawings that someone—him, probably—had tried to scribble out. Snickering at his attempt to make a dick look like a moose, I stood and handed him his crutch. He was no taller than me and not any stockier, but his shoulders and arms were more muscled.

"I'd say the crutch is what made you look feeble," I said as he tucked his support under his armpit. That got me a wry glance, which really worked well on him. The man was fine, no doubt. "I'm kidding, really. They're trying to find the funding to make the rink more accessible, but money for hockey barns isn't as easy to raise as it is for the football stadium."

"In *Minnesota*? The only people who love hockey more than Minnesotans are Canadians."

"Well, tell that to the fundraising committee," I replied, hoisting my skates back to my shoulder. "You good to go now, sir?"

I yanked the door open, and hot, humid air blew into my face. Ugh. I was not a fan. And my new bedroom had no air-conditioning.

"I'd be much better if you'd stop calling me 'sir.'" He hobbled through the door, giving me a fast up-and-down as I held it open for him. Okay, so he was either into guys, which made that spark in my belly begin to glow like an ember someone was fanning, or he was sizing me up to take a swing. "No one calls me that. Everyone calls me Ethan, or if you're an ex of mine, asshole, but never 'sir.' That's my dad."

I chuckled as he maneuvered out into the late summer evening. "Okay, Ethan, do you need help to your car?"

He paused just outside the rink, a breeze tugging at his

short brown hair, and gave me a look that dripped with sarcasm.

"Thanks, kid, but I'll be fine." I nodded. Someone ran past and shouted to someone else. We stood there staring at each other. "You know what I *could* use some help with?" I shook my head, my attention on that scar on his eyebrow and how the dark hairs of his expressive eyebrows didn't seem to grow on that short white strip. "The door to that coffee shop over there."

He tossed that sexy chin toward The Aviary. "Oh, yeah, okay. I can get you seated in there no problem, Ethan."

The smile he flashed me was glittering white. A dimple popped out. I felt myself flush, the warmth under my skin pleasant and tingly. This Ethan was just the kind of man who always grabbed my eye. Mature, sassy, strong, and sure of himself. My blood hummed.

"Thank you…" He let it dangle.

"Benoit," I answered, extending my hand.

"Ah, so one of those Canadians we were just talking about?"

"Yes, sir, sorry." The heat in my cheeks deepened.

"Yep, should have known by your incredibly attractive politeness."

He rocked around on his crutches and slid his palm over mine. His hand was warm, his grip sure, his fingers long and scarred, rough from working hard.

Bet they'd feel incredible running up the inside of your thighs.

Oh, hell yeah, they would.

Fuck. No. No. No.

"Right, uhm, so inside we go." I ran from Ethan to The

Aviary, yanking on the door so hard it was a miracle it didn't rip off the hinges.

Ethan made his way over, giving me the oddest glance as he turned sideways and thumped into my hangout. Thankfully, the place was pretty empty. The staff was just rolling things out in preparation for classes starting tomorrow. The heady smell of brewing coffee reached me, making me yearn for a cup. I'd become horribly addicted over my years here on campus, and according to Jacob and Hayne, come the end of senior year, it would be the only thing keeping me functioning.

Ethan stood just inside the door, assessing me rather openly. "Why don't you join me for a cup? My treat to thank you for your kindness to a wobbly old man."

The *thump-thump-thump* of my pulse in my ears was a warning that this man right here was not at *all* on the agenda. Studying and hockey. That was it. No flirting with sexy older men, no staring into pretty blue eyes, or admiring the way his biceps flexed and bunched as he hitched along on his crutches. No. No. No.

"I have to go do... this thing." I waved a hand in the general direction of Saturn, ducked my head, and bolted like a greyhound. No shit, I ran all the way home, my skates bruising my back.

"Dude, it's like a hundred and forty out there. Why are you running?" Ryker asked when I exploded through the front door. He was in shorts and sucking on a juice box.

"Just had to get some distance between myself and temptation," I muttered, hiking up the stairs to my room.

Ryker followed, chattering away about chicken fingers. The man could wax poetic about chicken for days. I was not in the mood to hear his dissertation on which chicken tender meal had the best sides.

"… Jacob that it really comes down to the spices used in the batter."

I nodded and shut my bedroom door in his face.

"*Dude!*" he gasped on the other side. I opened the door a crack.

"Sorry for being rude." Damn my courteous Canadian heart. "I just, uh, need some time to meditate."

"Oh, cool, yeah, sorry. Goalie mind stuff. Got it." He flashed me a smile that made hearts all over campus flutter. "Your mail." He handed me several envelopes after tapping his brow with them. A soft pink envelope drew my attention. Probably some sort of ad from that store in town where I'd bought hair care products. I tossed them all aside to deal with later.

"Thanks." I smiled back and eased the door shut slowly. Once I heard Ryker going down the creaky steps, I kicked off my sneakers, placed my tiny squirt bottle on top of the little dorm fridge in the corner, stripped to my briefs, turned on the fan, and threw myself onto the bed. The sun was far from setting yet, and I was too agitated to nap. I could have meditated or done some yoga to loosen up the tension in my shoulders, but that would have been too sensible.

Instead, I pulled up a streaming app and began watching *Mad Men* because Jon Hamm in those 60s-style suits made me straight up bug nuts. I binged a whole season, the only thing pulling me from my Don Draper adoration was when the people in the attic—Hayne and Scott—decided to start sexing it up while some classical music blared. I rolled my eyes to Drake hanging over my bed.

"Some people have some terrible taste in mood music," I muttered just as Hayne cried out that he needed something deeper. I didn't lie there listening to the rest. Within seconds, I had my earbuds in and was deeply involved in some wild fantasy that involved me and Don Draper. Things started out okay, but somewhere along the way, as I worked my dick with more and more speed, Don morphed into Ethan with the blue eyes. Ethan was smoking a cigarette as I blew him, his hand resting on my face, his sapphire eyes hooded.

Joan Holloway was there, in a red dress that did all manner of wonderful things to her sultry figure, taking notes while I tried to cram Ethan's dick down my throat.

"Don't forget your ten-o'clock meeting with Coffee Bright Coffee Filters, Ethan," Joan said, her legs crossed and her high heels as red as her lips. "Oh, and why don't you fuck him now? I think that would be what the customer would like to see in the ad copy."

"Yeah, fuck me, Ethan," I panted around the cock in my mouth, wondering if someone were sketching out a commercial with this blow job featured in the drawing. If so, I bet they'd sell a lot of coffee filters.

"I'll fuck him when he learns what's important in life," fantasy-Ethan said, all growly and two-pack-a-day smoker voiced. He patted my cheek and took a swig of the whiskey that had miraculously appeared in his hand.

My balls drew up. I hurried to grab the base of my dick, but there was no stopping the orgasm. I thrashed around in my bed, gasping and sweaty, one earbud lying on my shoulder so that the whimpering mewls of Hayne being driven over his own precipice slid into my ear. I shuddered and rolled to my side, briefs soaked with spunk, back slick with sweat, Joan of the red dress and amazing figure shaking a well-manicured finger at me inside my head.

"You really need to focus, Father Morin," Joan chastised before she and Ethan dissipated into nothingness.

"Okay, no more thirty-something guys in suits and fedoras," I panted as I pulled the pillow over my head to drown out Scott hurtling toward a blown nut. It was going to be a long, long, *long* year.

CANCELING my subscription to that streaming service helped me rediscover my monk status. How weird was I that I stroked off to some show about ad men instead of over online porn like everyone else in the world? People say we goalies are odd, and sometimes I balk at that. There's nothing odd about wanting pristine ice under your skates. There *may* be something odd about tugging one off while you fantasized about some guy you met once wearing a hat and sipping whiskey while you sucked him off. It had been two weeks, and Ethan and his blue eyes were still trying to seduce me in the night. But my iron will was now totally in control.

"Sex drives are for wimps," I whispered as I hunkered down into my butterfly stance, our first official team scrimmage about to begin. September had stolen in uneventfully, the stickiness of August easing day by day. Our first game wasn't until the end of October, against the Buffalo State Badgers, but we were still on the ice daily, as we were now in-season. Training, working, on-ice time with the team and alone with our goalie coach, this all added to a full schedule of classes. Now, I also had two days a week in a local elementary school as a pre-student teacher—or a practicum—under the guidance of a mentor teacher. I'd done my first day just yesterday, and as nervous as I'd been, the second graders had been amazingly welcoming.

The first puck fired at me went wide, and all thoughts of instructional methods, TV dramas, and beautiful blue eyes faded from my mind. I locked down on hockey, on the hiss of a puck flying at me, the slice of my skates as I shifted to throw up a blocker, the thud of a frozen chunk of rubber hitting my chest at over eighty miles per hour. The pucks kept coming, and I found that place that goalies go to in their minds. It's a tight place; nothing is admitted into it unless it's the soft sound of water, spring water that dribbles into the lake, feeding it as the ice crusts over the surface, thickening, holding me up as I breathe in air so cold it scorches my lungs. That is the place where I go, hockey at its core, pond hockey back home on that tiny circle of thick ice.

Ryker tried, and he failed. I threw him a look as he skated around my net.

"Head standing right there!"

I nodded at his compliment and then locked my sights on the next man coming at me. The puck on his stick, the rush of his breath, the slight way he moved his shoulder to try to pull me into going left, all of that fed into my brain in a millisecond. Then he pressed down on his right foot, and I knew he was going to take the shot early. The puck was launched from the blue line, his stick bending nearly to breaking. I threw up my catcher, snapped the puck from the air, and rolled my hand down and over, showing the team the puck resting there snug as a bug.

"I am a brick wall!" I shouted at the Eagles, and they all hooted and whooped.

Yeah, this was my year. Nothing was going to distract me. Absolutely nothing.

After the last man had taken his shot, we broke up for some light work with our respective coaches. Sam Gagnon and I did some paddle work with Coach Upton, nothing too heavy, just the basics to ease us back into the proper mindset. Our goalie coach was top-notch and never lost his temper or yelled. He was beyond patient, especially with the freshmen who were trying out for the team. Sam and I were both seniors and would be gone in May. There had been a lean couple of years for goalies, but this year we had five who were trying out.

They didn't worry me too much. I was the starter and would remain so throughout the season. My eyes were firmly locked on the prize: the Owatonna Eagles traveling to Detroit and winning the Frozen Four championship in April. Then graduation, followed by summer hockey camp and the Edmonton training camp. I had to make sure I got this team to Detroit and the championship.

I plodded down the chute, listening to the sounds of the Eagles locker room growing louder and louder as I neared it. Shouts and laughter, "Panic! At the Disco" playing on the old boom box. A roll of tape escaped the room. I stooped to pick it up and whipped it to one of the D-men in the corner after he went long. It was like coming home in a way. A small, pink envelope—another advertisement for Showers & Specialties probably—peeked out of one of my spare skates. Okay, that had not been there before. I threw a look around the locker room, trying to ferret out who the asshole was. Had to have been Ryker. Who else had access to my mail?

Stupid shit. Did he think I cared if people saw that I got sale ads from a bath shop? He needed his ass kicked. I yanked the envelope free from my skate, glowered at it, then ripped it open, hoping to find a damn web address where I could unsubscribe from junk mail and unwanted emails. Not that I didn't love their line for men but—

I STILL LOVE U BEN * *SUMMER GONE BUT NOT ME* * *I BE HERE SEE U WATCH U LOVE U.*

THE FLOWERY PAPER was soft white, the letters written with bold red marker. My heart leaped into my throat. Was this a joke? My sight flew around the room, but no one was laughing or pointing at me. Still, it had to be someone yanking my chain. Ryker. Had to be. He'd seen the advertisement and…

What? Decided to pretend he was some sort of psycho stalker fan?

"What the hell?" I muttered, balling the stupid prank up and shoving it into my personal bag. Dumb ass. I threw some tape at the back of Ryker's head. It bounced off his curls, and I got a seriously dark look. A dirty hockey sock was his retaliation. I stalked into the showers, not amused in the least, my pulse tripping over itself. Stupid ass. Probably he and Scott dreamed that up. Got Hayne to write that shit down in some stupid attempt at childish handwriting.

The showers were packed, guys talking about classes and women, cars, food, and the upcoming season. I dumped my shampoo, conditioner, and body wash out of the mesh bag I carried it in and soaped up, working the lather into my skin with a rough shower sponge. As much as I disliked shampooing more than once or twice a week, as it destroyed my already dry hair, after hockey practice, I had to. The rich golden shampoo was followed by a thick conditioner heavily applied to the top, which was a few inches longer than the buzzed sides. After that was rinsed off, I was out of the shower, wet feet squeaking in my green Crocs, clean towel around my waist, and my sopping wet bag full of shower gear in hand.

I heard Ryker shout my name as I stepped out of the shower area into the dressing room. As I turned to reply with my middle finger, my mouth snapped shut when my gaze and Mr. Blue-Eyed Ethan's met across the rowdy room. His eyes dropped to where my towel was knotted right under my navel and then flew back to my face, his head inclining just a fraction of an inch. A wildfire broke out inside me as Ethan continued to talk to our defensive coach as if they were old buddies.

I swallowed. He smiled and I suddenly had a massive need to see him with a tumbler of whiskey in his hand, fedora seated jauntily on his head, as he beckoned me to kneel before him and take him into my mouth.

I groaned inwardly at the loss of my poor, easily beguiled scruples.

FOUR

Ethan

"ARE YOU EVER GONNA GET RID OF THAT THING ON YOUR face? Because you look like shit."

I turned away from the temptation of the twenty-two-year-old goalie and faced one of my oldest friends in the world, the one who'd gotten me to volunteer at Owatonna U. in the first place. Isaac Upton, or Downer as he'd been called in his NHL days, was a friend from way back. Right back to pond hockey in his mom's backyard at the age of six, long cold days where hockey was all we had to think about. We'd both been drafted, me to Boston, him to Calgary, but a puck that had slipped up and inside his helmet left him with a vision issue that had cut his time in a professional net far too short. He was married, with kids, all settled in Owatonna, goalie coach to the university team and freakishly happy with his life. Despite the ten years playing professional hockey I had on him, I envied his life more than a little.

"Are you even listening to me?"

"Sorry, what?"

"This"—he tugged forcefully at my full beard what— "what look were you going for with this? Early caveman?"

"Oh, that."

After crashing out in the third round of the Stanley Cup, during which guys traditionally grew lucky beards, I'd had major burnout. It was the moment where I should have realized I was already harboring thoughts of hanging up my skates. It was obvious when all my teammates had shaved, ready for vacations and summer training, and there was me letting my beard grow. I was pretty sure it was my subconscious telling me that I didn't need to shave because I was considering being done with professional hockey, and I could hide behind my beard. Add breaking my leg, and I genuinely considered it true that fate wanted me to face new life choices. I wasn't the most superstitious of sports people out there, but I did have a strong belief in destiny. After all, I could have broken my leg anywhere, but the fact I did it in my home town was one hell of a statement. Still, the concept of not playing, of giving up on a career that had been my whole life was possibly the most frightening thing I'd ever considered.

Could it be time to put family first? Settle down? Do something more with my life?

Isaac was still tugging at my beard, and I brushed his hand away. "Fuck you, Downer. I'm rocking Chris Evans in *Infinity War*."

He looked at me blankly; he clearly had no idea what I was talking about. I decided there and then to organize film nights in the future where I shared the *Avengers* goodness with my friend. Of course, once he saw the bearded Evans, he would see my beard was long past tidy.

"I don't know what the fuck you're talking about. But

right now, you look like a... what's that thing called in that film you like? The one with that big hairy ape thing."

"Which film?"

He snapped his fingers. "I got it, Star something, and you look like a big ass hairy Wookie." He seemed so happy with himself at the lame chirp I *almost* didn't call him on it. But then, I wouldn't have been a hockey player if I didn't chirp back.

"Says Yoda on a bad day," I quipped. Of course the reference was lost on him, and I rolled my eyes and added *Star Wars* to the movie list. I'd already thought about going somewhere and getting the damn beard fixed; maybe to a place with hot towels and soothing music because the thought of wading through the jungle on my face alone in my bathroom was daunting.

"Whatever, dude. Wookie is all I'm saying." He turned to face the rowdy room full of seniors and cleared his throat. "Okay, guys, settle down." The volume was still high, so he put his fingers in his mouth and whistled loudly. Finally everyone was quiet and looking our way. I think most of them hadn't seen me standing there in the corner, and I noticed a couple of them do a double take when they saw me. Particularly Ryker Madsen, whose mouth dropped open, but then, he'd met me outside of hockey through his complicated link to Brady Rowe.

"I want you all to meet our newest volunteer coach—"

"That's Ethan *fucking* Girard," someone faux-whispered, and for a second I felt like a respected hockey player and not someone who'd lost his shine.

"—Ethan Girard," Downer continued, ignoring the whispers and open mouths. "D-man for Boston, holder of two Stanley Cup rings, two times winner of the Norris

Trophy. He's volunteering to look after our D-corp for a few months while his leg heals. This means I'll have more time with the existing goalies and the new guys coming up. Questions?"

Everyone started talking at once, but it was Ryker who talked the loudest, and it was him as captain the others deferred to. I'd actually nursed a small hope that one tall Canadian goalie would be the one who took point on all the questions, but he was slumped back in his stall, his arms crossed over his chest, staring at his feet. Seems as if he wasn't so happy an NHL professional was in the room with the team, or maybe it was the whole comment from Downer about the up-and-coming goalies who would be taking his place? Who the hell knew.

"You're really staying here with us?" Ryker asked the question I knew everyone would want an answer to. "What about Boston?"

"It's been fourteen seasons. I'm healing and considering my options—maybe it's time for me to get out of the way and give the young forwards on other teams the chance to actually get goals against Boston." I winked to underscore the comedy of that statement, and a couple of the guys snorted laughs.

"Hell, you can't give up on Boston," a tall skinny guy moaned loudly. "Just when I start thinking Bean Town has a chance again, we're fucked now." He sounded miserable, but I couldn't exactly give him positive news just because he was a fan of the team I'd played for. The R-word loomed over me, but every player has to retire eventually.

"I think they'll do okay without me for a while," I deadpanned, but tall, skinny kid wasn't happy. He muttered a soft curse and added something about Boston fucking it all up.

"Chill, Laffs," Ryker said and patted him on the head. "Boston will be fodder for the Railers anyway."

Laffs brushed his hand away. "Fuck you, baby-Mads."

Everyone laughed, easy camaraderie was evident in this room, the team a happy one. All except Benoit, who hadn't looked up from his feet. That could've been a goalie thing, I guessed. I'd seen some weird ass goalies in my time, steamrolled into a few of them on occasion when playing.

"Okay, so now Advisor Girard is going to say a few words," Downer said and nudged me in the side.

"I am?" *Shit, really?* "Oh, well, seems I am." I paused for a moment, checking out the room. "So, yeah, I haven't seen much in the way of game tape for the Eagles, but you ended third in the Big Ten last year and only narrowly missed out on the Frozen Four semis. I know we can manage the turnover in seniors leaving on graduation and get some solid points this year, with the aim of winning. I'll be talking to you all individually, even the forwards and the net-minders, to get a feel for what our D-corp is up to. Questions?"

Everyone had questions it seemed, ranging from what it was like winning the Stanley Cup, *the best day of my life and hard work*, to what I was going to do while I couldn't play, *work with you guys, for now*.

Tall, skinny guy's hand shot up. "Lafferty, second line D."

"Let's make this the last question," Downer warned. "Some of us have work to do."

I moved forward a little and shook Lafferty's hand as I

had every other person who'd asked me a question. "Nice to meet you, Lafferty."

"So my question is." He side-eyed Ryker. "When you played the Railers, February two years back, what did it feel like to stop that last breakaway from Tennant Rowe, meaning we beat the Railers into the ground?"

Someone snickered, and Ryker jumped Lafferty, and the two of them began rolling around on the floor in a fake fight. I left them to it, following Downer to the small office that was going to be my home. Sue me if I stole one last glance at Benoit, just to see if he was looking up yet.

He was. Right at me, with narrowed eyes and a mutinous expression. I don't know who'd pissed in his Wheaties, but just to fuck with him, I winked. Never let it be said that I played safe with a guy I was attracted to.

And yeah, I'm thirty-two; he's twenty-two. I have ten years on him, not to mention I'm a volunteer coach for his team. I'd just give anything to see him smile at me.

WEEK ONE WENT AS WELL as expected. The D-men were in flux since losing Jacob Benson, and it was obvious from the scrimmages that they were hurting with not having him there. Ryker was his usual scrappy self, but one forward does not a team make. I'd spent all of last night searching the stats for the beginning of their previous year versus the end, and one thing was also glaringly obvious. They had lost a forward midseason, a strong member of the team, and it had hit them badly. We talked about my impressions in the coaches meeting.

"You lost Scott Caldwell to steroid abuse. It impacted your lines."

Rick Gardner, forwards-coach and an all-around nice guy nodded. I'd been pleased to find out he wanted to work *with* me as opposed to *against* me. I loved that about the Eagles: not one person was territorial. If a D-man wasn't getting in the right place or a forward wasn't crisp in his passes, the whole team, plus coaches, gathered around them and worked it out. This was the kind of growth and grit you'd see in a Frozen Four championship team, and it was a good start to the work we needed to do.

"Big-time. He was on Ryker's line; it threw the entire team."

"You think he'll come back after his suspension?"

"I don't know. The door is always open. He's feisty and was good on Madsen's line." Gardner shrugged. "Damn shame what happened to him. Lost his brother, lost his way, but he's working with the little kids here, keeping his nose clean, and maybe we'll see him back. Who knows?"

After the meeting, I left the rink the back way, heading into town, hobbling at a slow pace off campus and following my map app to the nearest barber. It wasn't a big shop, but it held a stylist, a couple of empty chairs, and one man in a reclining chair with a towel over his face. The receptionist looked up from his keyboard, his eyes widening, and with a horrified expression.

"I know," was all I said.

He stood, dramatically gesturing to the nearest chair. "Sit down! Silvie! We have an emergency!"

The short, round, loud woman called Silvie didn't miss a moment to tell me how much better I'd feel as soon as I had my beard gone and any remaining stubble shaved off. She even talked me into having my shaggy mane of haircut. I can't actually recall the last time I'd had smooth skin or properly styled hair. In all likelihood, it had been for the team photos before last season. Even then, I'd been rocking designer stubble and hair I'd had to tuck behind my ears.

"There you go." I'd watched my face appear from under the hair, and the person who stared back at me was different from the one I remembered. That person had been a whole lifetime ago, secure and safe playing team hockey, and this new me was stateless and a little scared. I tipped generously and then didn't know what the hell to do next.

Until that was, I saw Benoit.

I'm a coach. Not his coach and I volunteer, but I'm a coach. I'm ten years older than him. But look at him. He's a man. He's so damn sexy. I wanted to stare into his gorgeous eyes and maybe act out on the attraction I'd sensed between us at our first meeting

"Benoit, hey," I said from across the street, watching him turn. At least he was looking at me this time.

"Hey, Coach Girard," he called.

I crutched over the road and stopped next to him. "Ethan. Outside the rink, call me Ethan."

He smiled at me, but the smile didn't quite reach his eyes, and he took a step back. I swear there had been a flare of attraction in his velvet brown eyes. But it vanished quickly, and he straightened his back.

"You..." He indicated my face by running his hand over his own smooth skin.

"Yeah."

This was one great conversation. *Not.*

"Anyway, this is me," Benoit said after a moment, then turned on his heel before heading toward a combination book shop and café called Gamble & James.

"Coffee," I blurted, having somehow lost all my faculties in the face of the strong, sexy goalie. "Would you like to have a coffee with me?"

Ten years dude. Coach. Player. Ten freaking years.

He glanced back over his shoulder. "I really need to collect the book I ordered."

Fuck my life. All these years I've played it cool, and I meet Benoit on no more than a handful of occasions, and I am smitten.

"Yeah? What book?" *What book? Why did I ask that?*

He stopped walking and turned to face me, checking a piece of paper in his hand and frowned. "*The Trauma-Sensitive Classroom: Building Resilience with Compassionate Teaching*, the second edition," he read, and that pretty much ended the conversation. This was insanely stupid. What would someone just starting out in life see in someone who'd done their time in sports and was now adrift and unsure about what he was doing next? I should've just walked away and left him be, but no, my mouth was running off before my brain connected.

"Teaching? That's your area of study?"

He smiled then, confidently, and my brain stopped working completely. I'd never felt a connection like this before, and I was the one to take a step back then because this could very easily get out of control. *You're attracted to him; just own it. See if he's interested.*

"Yeah, my ex-boyfriend's brother's friend was a teacher, and I'd listen to his stories, and I realized that was what I wanted to do."

"Boyfriend?"

He bristled then. "Yes. Why?"

I forced my hands into my pockets and exhaled noisily. "I'm relieved, but also… seriously, would you like to get a coffee? Or something more maybe. A drink? Dinner?"

His eyes widened, and I knew the moment I'd finished asking that I'd stepped over an imaginary line in the sand. Was it because I was a coach? I mean, I wasn't being paid. It was volunteering. I wasn't faculty. It wasn't against the rules. He liked dudes, I liked dudes, and okay, the age gap was there, but it was only ten years, and we were both adults.

"You mean like a date?"

"Just like a date," I said, and confidence flooded me in an instant. I took comfort in the fact he wasn't running in the opposite direction and that there was a softness in his expression. He half smiled, and I saw a hundred possibilities in that smile. I desperately wanted to kiss him, to taste him, and see if the heat that flared inside me was matched in him.

Abruptly the interested expression changed into serious focus.

"No, I mean, thank you, but I can't."

My heart sank. "Can't or won't?" I asked jokily, as if the fate of my entire day didn't rest on his answer.

He shook his head sadly. "Both."

I watched him go into Gamble & James, but I couldn't stand there staring through the window like a fucking idiot. So I called a cab from the next road up and headed home.

And I could hear my brother's laughing voice in my head, "Crashed and burned, bro, crashed and burned."

FIVE

Benoit

WHAT HAD MY LIFE BECOME? HIDING INSIDE A BOOK store, gaze glued to Ethan as he made his way to a cab. I closed my eyes, inhaled through my nose to ease the thunderous pounding of my heart, and exhaled slowly through pursed lips. How was it possible for the man to get any more gorgeous? That scruffy mountain man appearance had really done him a disservice because now, with his cheeks bare, his strong jaw really stood out. I drew another calming breath, trying to find focus amid a tornado of uncertainty. Maybe he should have kept working that ZZ Top look, even if it had done nothing for him. The new Ethan Girard had tangled me up like a fishing line. How had I not known him at first? Those eyes should have given him away. He was a damn legend here in Owatonna, hell, in all of hockey land, and I'd never made the connection. That stupid beard. It had hidden his face from me. Wish he had it back.

I spun from the window, back resting on a yellow brick

wall, and stared at the spines of books directly in front of me.

The Randy Duke of Dillington

Capture Me with Your Heart

Ride 'em Hard, Cowboy!

Great. I was hiding from my crush in the romance section. I pulled one of the books from the shelf, flipped it over, and was shocked to see two men on the cover. I glanced around, opened the book, read the interior and the blurb, and grabbed all seven of the novels in the gay cowboy series.

The lady at the register said nothing when I checked out. I shoved the books into my backpack and jogged home, the cooler air refreshing as it touched my overheated cheeks.

I paused at my front door as a thought hit me smack dab in the face. "I never got the book I needed for class!" I shouted to the heavens, pissed as hell that fucking Ethan Girard had rattled me so badly. That way he made me feel upside-down was getting to be annoying. Avoiding him was almost impossible. He was on the ice all the time, or in the locker room, or dallying around in the halls of the barn. You couldn't swing a cat without hitting Ethan Girard. And then he finds me in town and asks me to have coffee with him. Did he not get how fundamentally wrong that would be? How getting to know him better would make me want him more?

Ugh. This attraction to a coach—excuse me, advisor— was not part of the senior year plan. Hockey and academics. That was all I was supposed to be thinking about. He was outgoing and easy to talk to. Not that I did much talking to him, but others did. He laughed with ease, as I'd guessed, and seemed willing to spend as much time as was needed with any player who sought him out.

Everyone on the team raved about him. And I felt myself slipping in my resolve not to associate with him. The other day I had skated over to listen to him tell a story about some crazy Russian winger and a trip to Vegas that had ended with butcher hogs running amok on the Las Vegas Strip. Everyone laughed, including me, and our eyes had met and held way longer than they should have. I was now fantasizing about him at night as well as during classes.

Now I'd daydream about the small scar on his chin that was easily seen and could be touched with a finger pad if someone had the urge to know what it felt like. A small bit of soft amid an ocean of short stubble. Would he close his eyes as I stroked it? Maybe his breath would hitch, and I—

"No," I told my plump dick and stalked into the house, the smell of fried onions rich on the air. "Just no," I whispered, heading for the stairs as the sound of Hayne humming in the kitchen filled the first floor. It was a homey sound that reminded me of my mother when she cooked. Twisting my head from the steady litany of Ethan thoughts, I began to ponder on my father and how he was doing. School work beckoned, but since I hadn't gotten the required reading, I couldn't begin work on the paper we'd been given to write.

Maybe after dinner, I'd walk back into town and go buy the right book. For now, I snuck into my room, toed off my sneakers, and flopped onto the bed, my backpack at my side.

With my phone lying beside me on my pillow, I opened the first of the gay cowboy books, snickering at myself for being so damn lame that I'd bought a romance novel. I mean, really? Tamara read romances, young adult things that made her weep and wail. I'd never quite gotten into the whole *Degrassi* phenomenon, preferring to watch more substantial shows. And as for romance books? No, not my thing. Stupid really. Romance books. Gay romance books.

I chortled, gave the gay dark-haired man on the cover another look, and discovered that he resembled Ethan a great deal, right down to the stunning azure eyes.

"Huh," I muttered, cracked the spine loudly as I opened the book wide, and settled in to spend the next hour snickering and poking fun at the book.

A sharp rap on the doorframe startled me. I lowered my book just enough to see Scott lounging in the doorway, jeans and ratty T-shirt, smiling in at me.

"I'm reading," I snapped and buried my nose back into the paperback. I had to find out if Drew and Mike would ever stop this fucking dancing around each other bit they were engaged in. It was obvious to me and everyone else in Windy Willows, Texas, that they belonged together. I mean, that kiss behind the horse barn should have been proof enough for Mike, but no, he was being all stoic and alpha male, pushing Drew away because he was afraid and—

"… me? I said dinner's ready. Been calling you for, like, ten minutes." Scott tugged the book from my hand. I growled like a dog who'd just had his bone stolen. I made a lunge for it, but Scott danced in reverse, checking out the cover, then giving me a waggle of an eyebrow. "Wow, gay cowboys. Never knew you were into spurs and saddles."

"Fuck. Off." I pounced on him, using the bed as a

springboard. After a short round of playful pushing and shoving, Scott tossed my novel to me, his eyes dancing with devilment. "Go serve the food. I'll be right down."

"Got to find a bookmark?"

"I got your bookmark," I countered, flipped him a big bird, and then bent the corner of my current page over. Shouts of outrage from all the women in my mother's book club echoed through space and time. We thundered down the stairs, filing into the small kitchen where Hayne was dishing up some fried burgers topped with onions and mushrooms, a big tossed salad, and some raspberry iced tea in an icy pitcher filled with ice cubes. "No Ryker tonight?"

"Nope, he's got that late class," Hayne replied, taking a seat beside Scott after he forked a burger from the platter. "He won't be home until eight thirty, so he said to eat and he'd just grab something at the chicken joint in town."

"Oh right, man, I'd hate a two-hour class that late. I'm wiped by four," I said and slapped a skinny, kind-of burnt burger onto a fat sesame seed bun.

Scott fixed a bowl of salad for Hayne and then one for himself. Hayne poked at his food generally or didn't eat at all when he was in a creative mood, but Scott seemed to tend to his man well, making sure he ate, even if he wasn't really into it. I never had any problem eating. I was always hungry. I'd heard Ethan explaining to one of the rookies the other day that it takes a lot of fuel to run a high-performance machine.

Damn it, there he is again, Ethan Girard, pushing into my thoughts.

The meal was good—nothing fancy as none of us could really cook—but it was filling and relatively healthy.

Hayne took his salad up to the attic after Scott insisted that he and I clean up.

"He's not going to eat that." Scott sighed after Hayne pattered off, the back of his thin arms coated with green and yellow paint. "I'll have to make him a shake for a treat later."

"I have some bulk builder in the cupboard. Toss some of that in there with the ice cream and milk. Tons of protein." I flexed my arms, then kissed each thick bicep. "Give him guns like mine. You can use it too, start getting in shape for hockey when you come back."

I stacked the plates and carried them to Scott at the sink. The dishwasher still wasn't working, and the repairman had never come. Ryker's dad was not happy and had vowed to come out over the weekend to fix it himself. Ryker had expressed some concern over that, saying that his father didn't know a socket wrench from a soybean.

"I'm not coming back," Scott said as he cranked on the taps.

"Yeah, right." I snorted while passing over the dirty dishes.

Scott looked at me, his expression placid, the aroma of lemon wafting up from the hot water filling the sink.

"I'm serious, Ben, I'm not going back to hockey."

My brain kind of hit a brick wall. I stared at him for a full thirty-seconds, the sound of water and the smell of dish soap telling me that yes, this was all real. I stuck my finger into the rinse water. It was hot. Right. So, I hadn't just hallucinated his reply.

"You're kidding, right?"

He gave me a soft shake of his head, then began rubbing a yellow sponge around the outside of a glass.

"No, I'm serious. I'm not going back to the team. I have to work on myself. It's only since I was suspended that I've begun to understand real happiness."

Even though he was telling me this in a tone that said he was deadly serious, I still couldn't force myself to absorb the reality of his words.

"But how? I mean, you've given so much to hockey. Trained for years; it was your dream."

"It was my father's dream and my brother's, but not so much mine. I can see that, now that I'm clean. I want to work with kids, love and take care of Hayne, and discover who I really am. For close to twenty-two years, I was the Scott everyone else wanted, and it nearly killed me. Now, I need to touch base with me for me. That make sense?"

A small cluster of bubbles floated up from the sink, popping midway between the water and the ceiling.

"Yeah, yeah, of course. But, man, I can't imagine walking away from hockey," I replied, my gaze returning to one of my closest friends.

"Someday you will. Hockey's not the be-all and end-all, my man. It's a game." I gasped and got a gruff chuckle. "I know, hard to hear, eh? But yeah, in the end, it's a game, and it'll leave you alongside the road like an unwanted dog. Ask any player over thirty-five, and they'll tell you how cruel a mistress hockey is, even for goalies. The real things, the things that matter the most, are being at peace and loving someone unconditionally."

I had no reply for him, so I merely nodded, stunned yet, and dried the wet glasses and plates he handed me. We didn't talk about it anymore after that. What was there to say, really? We chatted about classes, our shared enjoyment of some video game, and a new superhero movie we both wanted to see when it released. After the dishes were done, the counters and table wiped off, and the floor swept, I climbed the stairs to my room, classical music playing overhead. I fell onto the bed, belly to the mattress, and laid my cheek onto my crossed forearms.

The stairs to the attic groaned as Scott climbed them, and I heard low voices. Then the music was all I could pick up. It was soft music, kind of sad, and it led me to a weird place mentally. I'd never known a guy who'd willingly walked away from hockey. Sure, lots of older guys like Jared Madsen retired due to health reasons, or when their bodies just gave out. But someone like Scott, who had a real talent and would probably go far, just saying "Nope, I'd rather be with my boyfriend and teach kids how to skate" was a totally unknown entity in my world. All my friends lived and breathed the sport. We had to. It was the only way to succeed in a highly competitive field. We'd all spent hours and hours daily on the ice, going to summer camps, leaving our family to billet with some other hockey family in a faraway state, chosen our schools based not on the curriculum but on the prestige of the hockey program and which pros had graduated from that chosen college. Hockey required total commitment. It ate up men and marriages, stole minds and wrecked bodies, yet we loved it with all our hearts.

"Wow," I whispered to the night that was slowly falling over Minnesota.

I rolled onto my back to study the ceiling, trying to make some sense of Scott's decision. After ten minutes, I decided that I'd never be able to do what my friend had done, just walk away and be able to smile about it. Either Scott was a far weaker man than me or a far stronger one.

Listening to him and Hayne laughing over some silly thing as lovers do, as I lay in my bed alone, I was hard-pressed to say which one of us was the weak one and which the strong. Right then, I would've given up just about anything to share a soft laugh with someone special who possessed warm blue eyes and a sprinkling of laugh lines.

Anything but hockey, of course.

ONE OF THE coolest things that we at Owatonna U did every fall was a campus-wide game of zombies versus humans on Halloween eve. It was a tradition that dated way back into the sixties as an homage to the George Romero's classic zombie flick *Night of the Living Dead*. No one's sure who came up with the idea, but we all owe him a debt of gratitude. It's not often that you can shoot a professor with a Nerf gun and suffer no repercussions. Not all the faculty took part, mostly the younger educators and several athletic coaches. I was surprised to see Ethan Girard's name on the sign-up sheet inside The Aviary. He struck me as the type to get into running around campus yelling and shooting foam darts at people. The man had a love of life and enjoyed doing things that most people his age shied away from. But was he able to do this with his injured leg?

The past couple of weeks had been busy with classes and practice, gearing up for the first game of the season, and I'd done little outside of the rink or the library. I'd been good. Hockey and homework. That was Father Morin's mantra, and it was paying off. My grades were excellent and my focus on the ice amazing. I was making saves that shocked even me, during our scrimmages.

With the zombie-human showdown a week away, I had to stock up on my gear, so I'd taken a bright October Saturday morning off from working on grading second grade vocabulary work—part of my pre-student teacher duties—and walked into town to search through the old thrift shop that sat across from a trendy little bakery where all the OU students flocked to when they left campus. I was hitting Caroline's Cupcakes to buy one chocolate cupcake after I found some apocalypse gear. One. That was what I was allowing myself. Damn, but I was a devout monk. My body was my temple, after all.

Stepping into the secondhand shop, I paused to read the signs over the racks and racks of used clothing. Menswear was at the back next to a wall filled with shelves that held knickknacks, dishes, and old pots. The place had a smell; I couldn't place. Musty clothes maybe? Mothballs as well.

I was deep into old jackets, pushing hangers aside to try to find something in an XXL that would fit but wasn't in too good a shape. We *were* supposed to be taking part in an apocalypse, after all. Ratty and worn was the name of the game.

"Imagine bumping into you here." I knew Ethan's voice well by now. I heard it every damn time I jerked off, which was a lot, considering I was supposed to be emulating a monk or something.

I tried not to look to my left. I really did, but the lure of those laughing blue eyes was too strong. I was a weak monk. Someone should've taken away my pretend monk card.

There he stood, smiling at me, dimple and chin scar flashing, in a stupid old camouflage jacket with a missing pocket and a blue fedora resting on his head. I had a flashback to the damn Don Draper-Ethen Girard fantasy that I'd rubbed one off to again, just last night.

"That hat is stupid," I stated as I yanked a well-washed denim jacket off the rack and began jamming my arm into a sleeve.

"Oh, I don't know. I think it looks kind of dapper," he replied, then reached into my jacket, his hand sliding over my chest in a slow, provocative manner that sent sparks to my fingertips and toes. "Might want to remove the hanger first," he whispered as he tugged a wire hanger free from the sleeve I was battling with.

"I knew that."

He winked.

I seriously wanted to knock that stupid hat off his head. It made him far too sexy, as if he needed more damn sexy working for him. I hated how off-balance he made me feel. "Why are you here?"

"To get ready for the apocalypse," he replied casually, leaning back to rest a hand on his crutch while checking me over. "That look works. Denim jackets were very big back in the day."

"I knew that too." Ugh, I was lame. Lame and chirpless and warm in the face. I needed something witty and fast. "You're not going to last five minutes in the war game with that bum leg."

He glanced down at the cast he now sported, then back at me. "I'm hoping they put me on team zombie. I got the shuffle down." He spun around and began dragging his leg up and down the aisle while making some horrid zombie noises. I had to snicker at him. I mean, he was just too damn funny. An old lady browsing the dishes gave us both a dirty look, which made the whole undead dude in a fedora even funnier.

"See, I'll be a good zombie," he said after lurching back to me. "I like to bite people too."

Flames raced through me, setting fire to the big bundle of tinder labeled *desire* that I'd shoved into a corner. I wet my lips. Those sapphire eyes of his lingered on my mouth. The thrift shop and the disapproving old lady fell away into white noise.

"Biting is against the rules." I coughed up, caught in the fire that was now growing into something that might not be easily contained.

"Well, I'll only bite people I know, then. Like you, maybe?" he asked, his voice a low purr that acted like an accelerant to the inferno already raging inside me. "Nothing says 'I like you!' quite like spreading the zombie plague." I blinked, unable to reply for fear I'd utter something stupider than I already had. "Or we could go to the cupcake shop and bite some cupcakes."

"I like to bite cupcakes." *That wasn't stupid at all, Ben. My God, you dumb ass.* "I mean I like to bite sweet things." *Stop talking. Stop talking right now!*

"Yeah, me too." The air crackled between us. I felt cold and sweaty, hot and chilled, all at once. "Come on, let's go find some sweet thing to sink our teeth into."

He limped along, using one crutch in hand and his jazzy fedora on his head as all my resolve went up in smoke. The man had *such* a fine ass.

We are fully engulfed. Repeat, we are fully engulfed!

I was toast.

SIX

Ethan

EATING CUPCAKES, DRINKING COFFEE, AND SITTING opposite Benoit had been *the* most erotic experience of my entire damn life. The way he smiled, the animation with which he spoke about teaching, and the absolute dedication he had to hockey were intense. After an hour of soaking in his passion, I think I felt less than him in a lot of ways. I'd lost my passion for the game when it was pain and loss more than joy and wins. I wasn't even getting the ice time that I was used to now, and I knew that was because I was becoming less useful. Less fast. Less inspired. Just *less*.

Finished at the age of thirty-two when many in other careers were moving upwards was just something that people in professional sports had to deal with. Sitting opposite Benoit, though, had reminded me of the fire that still burned in my belly, a fire, which I hoped would carry me on to the next stage of my career.

He was so incredibly serious about his hockey, to the point where we spent most of the chat dissecting a highlight reel backhand glove-high shot I'd used in a game against Vancouver more than four years ago. Which proved two things to me. One, that he was a hardworking goalie who wanted to learn his craft. Two, that he had evidently looked me up on YouTube or had known about me before or whatever. It simply meant he was interested in me in a hockey way. Now all I needed to do was turn the spark of attraction between us into a flame. Because I wanted that interest to extend to us in a personal way and to taste him so badly.

When we'd left the café, hands brushing every so often as we headed back to the college, I'd been turned on, confused, lustful, tired, and utterly overwhelmed. And that had just been over coffee. Now, lust-filled confused-me was dressed as a zombie, complete with guts hanging out and fake decaying-skin makeup, taking cover behind the bench in the quad. How the hell was I going to handle the fact that Benoit had just hurdled said bench and was now only a few inches from touching me and taking me out of the game. He'd drawn the human-team straw, and when it came to me being part of the infected zombies, that was giving him an unfair advantage because he only had to shoot me, and I was done in the game.

He held up his Nerf gun.

"I have one," he called out, and Ryker vaulted the same bench, landing in a crouch and leveling the gun at me.

"Aha!" Ryker announced loudly. "One more down." I was actually pathetically grateful because fuck, my leg was sore, even if I was mostly just shuffling around. But even as Ryker went to shoot me, Benoit caught his hand.

"He's mine," Benoit announced. "I'm keeping him and running tests to find a cure."

That was some diversion from the script, which consisted mainly of half the participants trying to take the other half out.

Ryker side-eyed him. "You're what now?"

Benoit released Ryker's hand. "Trust me, I'm a world-famous scientist who can use this particular zombie to find a cure for the entirety of the human race." He said it so damn seriously, that Ryker and I exchanged glances. Then Ryker snorted a laugh.

"Goalies are fucking weird," he announced. "Later, Mr. Scientist." He ran off, letting out a blood-curdling yell, jumping groups of studying bystanders sprawled on the grass, and then vanishing around the corner.

Benoit raised a single eyebrow. "You coming quietly, advanced-zombie-who-can-think-rationally?"

"Is that what I am?" I asked and looked down at the fake entrails. "My guts are hanging out."

Ben poked at my chest with the Nerf gun. "But your brain is intact." He threw his head back and let out a manic laugh just like any crazy ass scientist losing his shit might do. I liked this Benoit, the one who forgot his focus and let out his inner child. I raised my hands above my head.

"I surrender."

Benoit leaned in. "And you agree to me experimenting on you?" He was all growling and up in my face, and I wanted to reach out, grab him, and kiss him right there, stage makeup and witnesses be damned. But if I reached out and touched him, I could win this face-off as part of the game, but fuck, I was so invested in whatever he wanted to do to me.

Jeez, I'm glad my entrails cover my erection right now.

"Uh-huh." That was pretty much all I could manage by way of an answer because fuck, Benoit was all kinds of hot and sexy and—

"Stand up," he ordered and stepped back and away, holding the Nerf gun on me. "I'm taking you back to our HQ."

I stood, using my crutches to steady myself, and he even held out a hand to help me before slipping back into character. He patted his pockets and frowned. "I don't want you knowing where our HQ is," he said and held up the gun. "Shut your eyes, zombie."

The thought of being blindfolded, of having Benoit run the scene, imagining me in bed, maybe tied up and unable to move, and I was leaking. All it would have taken was for me to carry that image to a private space, and I could jerk off in about three pulls. Hell, I might not have even gotten my hand on my cock. I shut my eyes as fast as was humanly possible or zombily possible.

"Turn around," he ordered and placed his hand on my arm, guiding me, reassuring me under his breath that it would all be okay.

All I could think was that it would be okay as soon as I had my alone time.

I wanted to open my eyes when my crutch hit something hard, but I forced myself not to, and he murmured the single word "door" before helping me up and over a step. We hadn't walked far, but I couldn't for the life of me think what door it was. Then he encouraged me backward, and I felt a wall.

"Can I open my eyes?" I asked, assuming we were still in character and that I was in the human HQ and that, probably, one of the team would be here as well, waiting for an explanation as to why a zombie had been brought back.

"No," Benoit said, and his voice was hoarse. I felt him shift, his hand trailing down my arm, resting on my hand.

"I'll be a good zombie," I teased, and I had more to say. This whole speech in character about how I could be the start of new zombie-human relations, hoping to go for humor, but he didn't let me talk.

Instead, he crowded me, his weight pushing me into the wall, holding me there. I was off-center, my eyes still shut, and then he cradled my face.

"Fuck," was all he said, and then we were kissing.

I didn't know if he wanted to guide this or if he wanted me to respond, but when he shifted a little and inserted his thigh between my legs to part them, I could feel how hard he was against me, and it was game over. He deepened the kiss, licking and sucking his way into my mouth, teeth clashing. I gripped his ass, trying to pull him closer, wanting him inside me. I'd never wanted to kiss someone so desperately, and I clawed at him as he held me still.

I was so close to coming in my pants, right there in wherever the fuck we were. The whole team could have been watching, and I wasn't able to stop. We were on fire, and I was burning up.

"BEN! Where you at?"

Ben pulled away from me. "Go away, Scott!" he shouted back.

"Why are you—?"

"Tomatoes," Ben interrupted.

"What?" Scott shouted. "Seriously?"

"You heard me. Tomatoes."

There was grumbling, but no more shouting, and I assumed Scott had gone. Then Benoit let out a huff of a laugh. "You can open your eyes now."

"I don't want to."

I want to do some more kissing, and maybe if you just put your hand on my cock, I could come.

He pressed a kiss to my lips and then nuzzled my nose. "Open your eyes."

So I opened them and tipped my head a little so I could kiss him as gently as he'd kissed me. I blinked as I checked my surroundings, the gloomy area under the stairs, away from prying eyes and far from being found out.

"What was that about tomatoes?"

Benoit smiled then and stepped away from me, losing the weight of him leaving me bereft. "It's a code word from when we were first met, me and Scott, and it's morphed into a 'don't come near right now I'm *busy.* '" He cupped my face again, looked so serious.

"What?" I asked because it seemed as if he was going to say something really important.

"We're doing this, then," he murmured.

"I want to. Do you want to?"

He took my hand and pressed it to his chest. His heart was beating so fast, the same as mine.

"Yeah. We should… I don't know… go out or something." He wrinkled his nose. "Although I have so much work right now, and I need to get my time in at the rink. I don't know how I'm going to—"

"Shhh." I wiped some of the luminous paint from his dark skin and then smiled at him. "I'll work with you at the rink. Tonight we work on your glove hand and also get to kiss some more? It's a win-win scenario."

He nodded, then stepped away so he was out of reach. The more familiar serious-Benoit was back, and I so badly wanted to tug him into my arms and kiss away the frown.

"What is it?"

"You're… I mean… what will people say?"

"*People* don't have to know right now. We'll play it by ear and keep it to ourselves if that's what you want?" He didn't say anything, so I forged ahead. "I'm not paid by the college. I'm a volunteer, okay? I can pull away from the team if it worries you. I don't have to volunteer."

Benoit moved back a couple of steps until he met the wall and then he leaned there, staring at me. "It's not that," he said, so softly I had to strain to hear.

"What is it?"

"It's not all rainbows out there, you know, the Railers. They have these guys, and other teams they have pride night, they tape their sticks, they make a show of being supportive, but Ryker says that Tennant Rowe puts up with some real shit. What if…" He stopped talking, and I could see him worrying at his lower lip with his teeth.

I'd witnessed the kind of insults thrown at Ten. Not by everyone, certainly not by the Boston team, but yeah, casual use of hateful words was rife. He dismissed it, worked it to his advantage, getting the guys who threw it at him all riled up by pretending not to hear them. As to the arenas, the only really bad one was the Raptors, but that had to be something to do with Aarni Lankinen, the asshole who'd taken Ten down.

No one liked the Raptors anyway.

"Talk to me," I pleaded because I wanted to make

Benoit's world safe, and I didn't know where the hell that came from, but it was an emotion I was pulling up from deep inside.

"Look, it's like this. Imagine I'm in net, right, and it's in overtime, and I have two skaters coming right at me, but I'm angry because they've thrown slurs at me all night, and I doubt myself, and I've lost my head space, and they get a puck by me, and suddenly they've won."

Realization hit me at what he was saying. "You don't just mean winning the game, do you?"

Ben kicked back with his boot, and it clanged on the old radiator, which was a solid shape in the gloom. "What if I'm not good enough to stay in the zone?"

The times I'd heard a skater say that, forwards, defense, goalies, coaches with years of experience, *what if I'm not good enough?* Self-doubt was a vicious circle, and I could see it poking at Benoit as he shook his head a little.

"Okay, so you're saying you want to keep this quiet because if teams knew you were dating a guy when you were at NHL level, then they could exploit what you think might be a weakness?"

"No, it's not a weakness. But I mean, I'm not lying to anyone. I've had boyfriends, but I don't want to make a big thing of… Yeah, I think so." He sounded so confused

"I've been in the closet for so long I sleep in the Narnia snow," I joked, but I was so badly torn. I wanted to tell him to be himself. I wanted that for him and, selfishly, for me. I think I really wanted to come out of hiding, make my mark supporting a team like the Railers.

Make a difference to inclusion in the world of professional hockey.

I also wanted Benoit, more than I'd ever wanted anyone.

But I understood him, and the part of me that listened and agreed ached with the pain of it all. I had ten years on him, I'd seen so much, and I was ready for the next step. He was just starting out, had a long time as a goalie ahead of him.

He cleared his throat. "And you're ready to come out, Ethan, to be the man you want to be and make your mark as a gay athlete."

"Bi," I corrected him as gently as I could, "and maybe that is what I want to do, but right now, I don't know anything about anything." The future was this nebulous thing that I hadn't in any shape or form pinned down yet. "Right now, I want to kiss you, I want to watch you on the ice and kiss you some more, I won't make a big thing of it, but right now, that is what I want."

He appeared to consider my words, then nodded. "I'll meet you on the ice. I'll text you later." Then he picked up his Nerf gun from where he'd let it fall and shot me dead in the center of my chest. "You're dead," he said. Then with a whoop, he ran up the stairs and left me there.

Little asshole.

THE ZOMBIES LOST to the humans, which was inevitable as we weren't allowed to run much, and the humans were made up mostly of the men's hockey and the women's basketball teams, which meant that hurdling and jumping and generally beating zombies was a thing.

The after-party was good though. Makeup and entrails be damned, I was happy to stand with a couple of the sports advisors, talking shit about hockey and soccer, basketball, and even touching on baseball. My eye kept being drawn to Benoit, his skin clear of the paint that had rubbed from my face to his, and he was very deliberately not looking at me. None of us were drinking, well, not to excess anyway, but it was a fun party full of heroic exaggerations of how the humans had won, alongside sad stories of all the dead zombies.

As the party was breaking up, I caught Benoit's gaze on me, but I didn't react. I promised him we'd keep this quiet, and I meant it.

Even on the ice later, after dark, just the two of us, me balancing to hit pucks at him, talking through my thoughts on angles as I did, and him stopping all but three shots, I acted appropriately.

Of course, as soon as we had privacy, I would kiss him so damned hard.

Privacy and kissing and *more* couldn't come fast enough.

SEVEN

Benoit

I REMEMBER WHEN I WAS YOUNG AND LEARNING TO STAND on skates. My father was always close at hand, encouraging me, telling me that skating was like life. It was all about finding balance.

Ever since I'd taken Ethan as an undead hostage, my life had become radically unbalanced. Kissing him had been a madness that had consumed me, much like a zombie plague, making me act not based on reason but based on primal urges. Instead of focusing on hockey and school, I was now wholly attuned to Ethan, his touch and his taste, the way he smiled, the stupid jokes he told, everything was Ethan. How I'd managed to keep my grades from slipping was anyone's guess. Thank the hockey gods our first game had come before that fateful night when the dead had been walking around the campus.

Our last game had been a shambles. We'd lost to a rival from Minnesota, the Duluth Diamondbacks, a much less skilled team. I carried a lot of the weight of that loss, not all of it, surely, but a goodly amount. It was obvious that the team missed Scott and Jacob, and the freshmen were trying, but they'd just not jibed on their lines yet. But all of that was secondary to my responsibility. The goalie is the last line of defense. And I had been sloppy.

Stupid plays had plagued me throughout the game, moronic choices because I was weighted down with school and a relationship that was burning so white hot the mere thought of Ethan made me shiver with want and grow hard. I'd been loose in my crease, unable to tune myself to the pulse of the game or even handle the puck well. Generally, I was to be trusted with the puck, skating behind my net to shove it to a teammate or send it down the ice. Not last night. I'd tried to grab the puck and pass it around the dashers to Ryker. Instead, I fumbled it, and it ended up on the stick of a Diamondback who'd pushed it into the empty net. The fucker then celebrated right on my blue ice. I shoved him off my ice, called him names that my mother would've been shocked to hear coming from her baby boy, and poked at the puck in the net with my stick. That loss was tough. The team as a whole had been demoralized. I'd sent Ethan a text after I'd showered saying that I was in no mood to be social. He'd understood. He was, after all, another ice rat. I'd spent the next day, a Sunday, lying around in bed until the sun rose until Ryker raced in without knocking.

"Get dressed. We have to catch a train to St. Paul to get to the game on time!" He ran back out of my room and thundered up into the attic, shouting about trains and Railers.

Scott bellowed at him to leave. Ryker laughed madly. I rolled to my side, not sure if going all the way to St. Paul for the Harrisburg-Minnesota game was what I should do.

I had schoolwork, and I needed to think about this thing with Ethan.

"Dude, seriously, get the hell up. We have, like, an hour!" Ryker yelled as he raced past my open door. The door he'd not shut after he'd barged in. When I didn't reply, he jogged back into my room, threw a sock at my head, and then when I still lay there like a lump, he dumped my hamper over my head. That got me moving. I threw the covers aside and wrestled him to the carpet, jamming a pair of dirty briefs into his face. He bucked me off, and we both lay there, gasping, staring at the ceiling.

"Ben, buddy, we need to do this. That loss last night was…"

"Demoralizing?"

"Well, yeah, but this will help get our heads on straight. Look…" He sat up and gazed down on me. "Neither of us is where we need to be mentally. I miss Jacob so much it hurts, way down deep in my soul, and I know you're trying to juggle this thing with Ethan."

"How do you know about Ethan and me?" We'd been super secretive, keeping our public personas as friends only.

"Dude, everyone on the team knows. I mean, the way he looks at you and how you gaze at him whenever you're both in the same room or on the ice? A man would have to be blind not to see it."

"Great," I huffed, covering my eyes with my forearm. "It's supposed to be on the down low because… well, for a lot of reasons."

"Whatever. I'm just saying you're tangled up as I am. Dad got us tickets. Let's take a day off from hockey, romance drama, and fucking essays and just go to the big city for some fun. Dinner after the game with my dad and Ten? A night at a hotel in St. Paul, train back tomorrow after brunch? Sounds pretty tasty, eh?"

"We'll miss all our Monday classes," I reminded him.

His face screwed up. "You sound so much like Jacob at times. Fine, let me lay this out in front of you. You'll be right behind Stan's net for two periods." My arm slid off my eyes. Ryker was smiling down at me. "Yeah, that's right. You can sit there and study one of the greats. Maybe even sit down with him and talk goalie stuff over dinner, so this would, in all actuality, be a work trip."

"What, you planning on claiming it on your taxes or something?"

Ryker snorted and slapped me hard on the chest. Bare palm to bare chest, the slap hurt like hell. "I just might. Are you in? Come on, say you're in. Scott and Hayne are coming…"

Getting a chance to watch Stan Lyamin do his thing? Yeah, there was no way I could turn *that* down. I nodded. Ryker hooted, then shoved a stinky sock into my face before springing to his feet and racing to the shared bathroom to shower and use all the hot water first.

THREE HOURS LATER, the four of us were seated at the away end of the Minnesota rink, right by the glass, surrounded by fans in evergreen jerseys while we were in dusky blue. No one had tossed beer on us or hurled a hot dog in our direction, but we did get some dank looks. I left my seat during warm-ups, as many did, and pressed my nose to the glass, eager to watch Stan preparing for the game. A girl with blue hair who was maybe sixteen was beside me, waving at Ten every time he skated past. Finally, just before the teams left the ice, Ten picked up a puck on his stick and tossed it over the glass to her. She cried. I mean, literally wept while holding that puck to her breast.

"The girls do know that Tennant is gay and married, right?" I asked Ryker when I was back in my seat, unable to really home in on Stan as there were too many screaming Ten fangirls to contend with.

"Oh, yeah, sure. Want a nacho?"

I shook my head at the proffered box of cheesy corn chips. I glanced past Ryker at Scott. He and Hayne were smooching, not a care in the world that people were milling around them. I was beyond confused as to how to proceed with life. The game pulled me out of my internal melodrama, the Railers crushing the home team with a shutout for Stan and four points for Ten—two goals and two assists—in the 5-0 trouncing. We waited outside the away locker room, in a small office, until Jared and Ten poked their heads in. Ryker gave his dads a hug, we all shook hands, and then we were carted off to a luxury hotel with a personal driver Ten had arranged, as he and the team were on a charter bus.

The afternoon tourist traffic was thick as we left the arena. The hotel was a towering building. I glanced upward as we lingered on the sidewalk, soft flakes of snow drifting down to land on my cheeks. Flags from around the world snapped overhead. Ryker tugged me indoors, and we hustled to the dining room to wait for the team. It was a huge room with soft blue walls and tables already set up for the Railers. The double doors were wide open in anticipation. Servers hustled in and out from a side door, setting up tables with glasses, dishes, and flatware. The rich aroma of beef cooking filled the private dining room. Sipping soda and chewing on crackers, we passed the time talking about the game. When the guys appeared, the lobby kind of went from mundane to hectic, fans milled around the players, shoving papers and hats at them.

I glanced from the hubbub to Ryker. "Someday, that will be us," I said to Ryker, and he nodded, his expression one of guarded optimism. Scott muttered something that Hayne kissed away, and although I wanted to ask, I didn't because I suspected Scott would always have some regrets about leaving the sport. Or maybe that was me projecting.

Within minutes, the dining room was packed with hungry hockey players. Food was being brought out and placed into warming bins. Rare roast beef, seasoned chicken, sour cream and onion mashed potatoes, green beans, bowls of fruit, cottage cheese, and massive platters of raw veggies with small dishes of dip. Water, soda, or coffee were continually filled by staff in white slacks and red tops. I returned to the table to find Stan seated beside my empty chair, his husband on his right. Ryker was still at the buffet tables, chatting away with Adler and Jared. Ten roamed up and down the food tables, picking and choosing, laughing at something Dieter had whispered to him as he had passed.

"Come sit, we make goalie talk while we eat," Stan called, patting my chair. I sat in a hurry, eager to make any kind of goalie talk I could. "Ryker tells me you have bad time with focus and concentration," Stan said as he buttered a round wheat bun.

"Oh, well, of late yeah." I placed my plate on the table and tugged my chair closer. "How do you do it?" He shoved the roll in, his cheeks round like a chipmunk, and stared at me as he chewed. "How do you put aside the life stuff when you're in the net? I thought I was on top of my game, but something sort of happened, and now I'm… it's hard to juggle it all. But you do, and I mean, you've got a husband and three kids. I've only got me and school. I guess I'm just…" I sighed and picked up my knife and fork. "I've got to win the Frozen Four this year."

"Is making big weight for carrying on young shoulders," he replied after he swallowed. "Winning is not just job of one player. Is all." He used his buttery knife to motion at the loud dining room. "Goalie mindset is tight, yes?" He tapped his temple with the knife. I nodded as I began cutting up my roast beef. "Good, then you must put other life things into places. Like nooks. Do you have nooks in brain?"

"I, uhm…"

Tennant, Ryker, and Jared sat down around us, Ryker steamrolling the goalie talk with the tale about Jared and the dishwasher repair job that had gone horribly wrong. Guess Stan and Erik hadn't heard it. Jared was less than impressed to be reminded of the smoke that had rolled and the sparks that had flown when he'd tinkered. And how we now had a brand-new dishwasher.

"Okay fine, so my skills lie in other areas," Jared finally said over the howls of laughter.

"I can second that." Ten chuckled with a wink and a kiss to his husband's cheek. I sat back, trying to figure out if nook meant something different in Russian than it did in English, and ate in silence, my gaze steady on Ten and Jared. They touched now and again, nothing too overt or over the top, but enough to let people know they were a couple. It was tasteful, not in your face. Subtle yet making a statement that observant eyes would pick up. Could I have something like that with Ethan? Could we be out and not outrageous? I roamed around inside my head for a long, long time.

"Hey, you going to eat that pudding?" Ten asked, jarring me out of a mental ramble.

"Fuck," I huffed, aggravated with myself that I missed everyone leaving the table to go back to their rooms and that I'd let myself drift so far from reality. Ten drew his hand back from the small dish of tapioca, smiling sheepishly. "No, hey, it's fine. Go ahead and eat it if you want."

"Actually, I'm full. I just came back because the team has retired, and you're sitting here looking like someone stole your dog."

I sighed and shoved the pudding to the center of the table. Servers were clearing off dirty dishes. Had I really drifted that long and that far? Obviously. No wonder my game was off.

"Stan said I need nooks in my head," I blurted out.

"Sounds like some of his advice. He probably meant you need to learn to compartmentalize." Ten leaned back in his chair, his green eyes warm. "Or he could mean you need to think like an English muffin. Hard to say at times." I snorted lightly. "Look, I know this isn't my place, but Ryker said you're seeing Ethan Girard but hiding it, and you're having a bit of a struggle on the ice."

"Ryker talks too much."

"Yeah, tell me something I don't already know. Thing is, I've been where you are now, right?" He stared right at me, his gaze serious. "Scared to come out because of what may happen to your career, dating an older man and terrified of what people will say about that, afraid of doing something but horrified of not doing something. That where you're at?"

"Right in the middle of that swamp," I confessed, then leaned up so that a passing server didn't overhear our conversation. "How did you handle it?"

"Man, I'm still handling it." Ten laughed wryly. "The media attention isn't as hot now as it was at first, but there are still some rogue asshole reporters or those with extreme viewpoints on the sins of homosexuality who pop up from time to time. Overall, though, it's been a good experience. Most people out there are decent. You think this thing with Ethan, who is one hell of a good guy, might be something serious?"

I thought back to the kisses and whispers, the nights hidden away at his place, and nodded.

"Yeah, I think it could be if I let it," I admitted, giving a young woman a smile as she passed by. "I'm just not sure I should. Maybe I should wait until after I've secured a spot on the team or won the Frozen Four or at least graduated. I just…" I blew out a sharp breath.

Ten leaned up and clapped me on the arm. "God, I recall feeling the same way. Look, I can't tell you what to do. That's got to be your call. For me, coming out was the only option because I didn't want to hide what Jared and I had. For other athletes waiting until they're more secure or retired is how they handle the whole *gay player* issue, as if being gay or bi or pan or trans should even *be* an issue when all we want to do is play…" He paused, took a cleansing breath, and then let it out as a quirky smile lifted his lips. "Sorry, it's a thing with me. Anyway, all I can offer as advice is to follow your heart." He thumped me on the chest, lightly, and then pushed to his feet. "Also, I changed my mind. I'm taking your pudding as a consultation fee."

"Go for it, dude," I replied and offered him my hand. We shook, Ten grabbed my pudding, stuck his finger in it, made a yummy sound, and ambled off to the elevators to join his husband for the night.

"Follow my heart," I mused, staring at the flowers in the centerpiece.

THE NEXT DAY I followed my heart. All the way home to Owatonna and to Ethan's front door. Hands clammy and shaking, I rapped on his front door, head up instead of tucked into my shoulders in case the neighbors saw me. It was kind of early, and Ethan tended to laze around if possible, so he was a sight for incredibly sore eyes when he opened the door. Sleep pants hanging off his hips, cheeks thick with scruff, hair rumpled from sleep, chest bare, tempting lips drawing up into a loving smile.

"Hey, I thought you wouldn't be home until later today." He stepped back and opened the door wider, giving the neighborhood an assessing look as I sauntered inside. "You do realize that everyone is up and getting ready for work?"

"Do not care." I grabbed him by the back of the neck, right there in the open doorway, and pulled his mouth to mine. He was stiff at first, but then as I licked along the seam of his tight lips, he began to loosen up. His hands slid around me, palms resting on my lower back, cinching me tightly to him. He was half-hard already. I kicked the door shut. He pinned me to it, his tongue gliding over mine, his grip on my back shifting to my ass.

"What the hell happened in St. Paul?" he asked when we broke for air.

"Followed my heart," I replied, slipping my fingers into his hair and yanking his lips back to mine. I lapped in deep, rolling my hips, my hard-on scrubbing over his now rigid prick. "Ten told me to, so I did. Also, there was talk about nooks. Oh man, I need more than this."

"'Nooks'?" Ethan asked as I shifted us around, using his gimpy leg as a means to lead a wobbly man to the sofa. "I'm still really confused," he admitted as he sat with a grunt.

"Russians," I panted, climbing over him, shoving my hands into his hair and fisting it. He arched an eyebrow as I covered his mouth with mine. God, but his taste was sublime. I sucked on his tongue, gyrating against him, humping madly until we were both on the cusp of coming undone in our pants. Ethan slid a hand between us, his blue eyes hot as he looked to me for permission to free our cocks. We'd never gone this far before. We'd kissed and petted, but I'd drawn the line at unzipping pants, hoping it would keep me on track for the really important things. Now I wasn't sure that this right here wasn't one of the most important things as well. It sure felt like it.

"Russian nooks? I'm still not following, but if it led us to this point, then I'll fill my house with Russian nooks, whatever the hell they are." I snickered and thrust against the back of his hand, my mouth gliding over his rough jawline, my lips abraded by his whiskers. "Are you sure this is what you want?"

"I'm sure." I pumped into him, nipping at his throat, my fingers wound tightly in his hair. "Touch me now."

Him tugging down my zipper sent shudders through me. In no time he had us both in hand, his cock pressed tightly to mine. My eyes drifted closed as he began to work us. When we needed slick, it was me who drew back to spit in his palm, my gaze dropping down to the sight of his fat dick and mine gripped tightly in his big hand. We were both cut. He was thicker, but I was a little longer. Pale and dark, slick cockheads resting side by side.

"I'm close," I growled, dropping my brow to his, eager to watch our cocks pumping out ribbons of semen as we bucked and snarled. Didn't take long. I shot before him, the heat rushing through me, out of me, all over his scarred fingers. The spunk eased the friction, made things wetter and noisier. Hotter.

"You're so beautiful," he murmured, biting down on my collarbone as his orgasm ripped him into bits. I held his head to my throat, my hips moving convulsively. He made some wonderfully sensual noises, low thrumming growls that pulled more wild tremors from me. Soon, though, the madness subsided, and his lips were roaming over my Adam's apple, his fingers easing up, our wet cocks growing soft. "You okay?"

"Mm, yeah, I think I am now." I leaned back a bit and gazed at him, my hands still in his unwashed hair. "This is what I want. Us, together. I don't want to hide it, but I don't want a presser to announce it either. I just want to discover us, play hockey, and try to graduate. Can we just be us until May? Are you okay with that?"

"Ben, I'm okay with anything that makes you happy and keeps you in my arms."

I smiled and kissed him hard and long. There was no guarantee that me taking this road would work out. We might crash and burn in a month, or we might go on to be something great, like Ten and Jared. Whatever happened, at least we'd be a couple, and we'd work through shit together.

"So, how about we shower and have something to eat? I'm so hungry I could eat... well, you." Ethan buried his face in my throat, bit down softly, and began giggling against my damp skin. "You up to being my next meal, human?"

"Shh, zombies don't talk."

"I'll die again if I can't talk."

"Don't think you can die twice, silly zed." I slid off his lap and helped him to his feet.

"Fine, I'll eat you quietly," he said as he led me to the bathroom.

He wasn't quiet when the feasting began, but then again neither was I.

EIGHT

Ethan

COACH QUINTON WAS PROVING TO BE DAMN ELUSIVE,
almost as if he knew I wanted to talk to him, but after
attempting to pin him down three times this day alone, I
finally cornered him by the gym doors.

"Do you have a minute, Coach?" He'd said I should
call him Bob, but my entire life had been hockey, and you
never disrespected Coach by using his first name under
any circumstances.

He gave a full-body sigh and shrugged. "I guess," he
said and then waited for me to talk. There was no way in
hell I was going to do this outside where anyone could
walk past.

"Can we talk in your office?"

He clapped a hand on my shoulder. "It's okay. I knew
this would happen."

"You did?" I couldn't help sounding bewildered. He
somehow knew I was going to talk to him about Benoit
and the whole Benoit-Ethan thing?

"Is it Boston? Did they call you back to coach? I heard

Vancouver wanted you as well, but that's just what the forums say, although there were others who said you'd be a perfect fit in Florida. That would be good, working with the other Rowe brother, but if I was you, and I'm not, obviously, I would stick with Boston because they know you there, and..." He shrugged again.

"I'm not going anywhere," I said. Then it hit me what he'd said. "Wait, Vancouver want me on their coaching team?"

"You can't always trust forums, but Slider98—he's a user from the West Canada group—says he heard his brother's friend..." He sent me a sheepish smile. "You don't need to know how I heard."

"Leaving Owatonna right now is not on my list of things to do." I spoke with complete confidence, although once I'd told Coach about the *thing*, then he might well consider a move to another country a good idea. Of course, if Benoit ended up where he wanted to be, then maybe I'd be joining Edmonton in some capacity or taking up a role within commuting distance. Hell, maybe I could even fully retire, live off my savings, and spend all my time fishing.

As long as it's near Benoit.

Where had that thought come from? We'd only been an official couple for two short weeks, but I was addicted to him, and he seemed more than just interested in me, and I wanted it to last past this final year of his at Owatonna. I guess that if the thought of being near him was that close to the surface, then maybe I should listen to my brain and begin making plans.

After today, after this awkward conversation with Coach Quinton.

"So you're *not* leaving Owatonna."

"No."

He looked confused. "But you don't want to work with the team anymore?"

"No, I mean, yes, I want to work with the team. Look… can we take this to your office, Coach?"

He led me through the double doors, past the gym, and up the stairs to his office, which was in a small section that jutted out over the ice. From his window, he could see the skaters, and right now, there was a group of little kids sliding around with their tiny sticks while a tall guy, on bended knee, guided their movements with gentle encouragement.

"That's Scott," he said and gestured at the man on the ice.

I knew Benoit's best friend worked at the rink, with the kids, and all the way up to the twelve-year-olds. I didn't know much else, because despite Scott being Benoit's best friend, he hadn't introduced us. Not that it was important, given we'd spent what little time we had together getting our sexy on, and kissing made talking difficult. I think we were in that selfish first flush of whatever we had going on because Benoit never talked about his friends much, let alone having a few moments for me to meet them. Hell, I didn't even know if the team knew about us. I didn't want to shout it from the college roof or distribute leaflets or stand on a corner and wax lyrical about what I and Benoit were doing, but the odd friend would be good.

After all, Brady Rowe was on speed dial, and he was my oldest friend in the world, and I couldn't wait for him to meet Benoit. I really needed to call him, but I knew I was putting it off while I thought long and hard about my future. I could imagine what he'd say; he'd push for me to go back to Boston, I knew it.

What would I do without the team? I'd been one of the lucky ones. I'd only played on one team other than Boston, and that had only been for a couple of years before I'd gone back. I liked to think I made a difference to that team, and I missed the guys so much it hurt. I'd left behind a family, and that was where my head was: grieving. The away games, cards on the plane, the charity events, the camaraderie that marked every single day, and knowing I could depend on the guys for anything, and all of that was gone.

For a few seconds, my nebulous decision to give it all up seemed the absolute worst thing I could do with my life.

"He's a good player," I commented when Coach looked at me expectantly.

"Yeah, he works well with the kids. He's a natural," Coach Quinton continued. "Have a seat and tell me what's on your mind."

I took the chair opposite the desk, and he sat in his own, and this felt better. This was less, Bob Quinton a friend, and more Coach Quinton, my sort of boss, who deserved honesty and respect.

"I wanted to talk to you about Benoit," I began, and he leaned forward in his chair.

"What? Is he okay? What's wrong? Is there something—?"

"Nothing's wrong, sorry," I interrupted.

He let out a strangled noise and sat back in his seat. "I've already lost Scott. I'm not sure I can handle losing my starting goalie as well."

"It's not that. It's a more personal thing." I steeled myself for explaining and then bit the bullet. "I've been seeing Benoit."

"'Seeing'?" He was confused.

"*Seeing*," I emphasized, and his eyes widened. "In fact, Benoit and I are in an exclusive relationship, and I wanted you to know so you can decide what you do next."

"'Next'… 'do'…" he repeated random words and then scrubbed at his eyes. "Okay, I can't see that…" More scrubbing, and then he pulled thick books from his shelf, the *NCAA Ice Hockey Rules* book and the *NCAA Ice Hockey Officials' Manual*. He flicked through the index and muttered to himself.

"Strive to have a positive relationship with players. That is all it really says, without going into detail. You're not a paid coach, but you still have a responsibility. So, okay, there's nothing in there that… really, you and Benoit?"

"Really."

"Well, that's not something… we've… you're not an official coach. He's a grown man, and I can't see how this will be against the team ethics, but I do have one concern."

"You're worried that if anything went wrong between us, that it will mess with his head and the team."

He smiled at me, then shook his head. "Not wholly the team thing. I like Benoit, and he's going to go far. He has sheer determination and a focused will. I'm more worried that if anything happens to end what you have between you, that it will impact his future. He's destined for big things, becoming an NHL starter. He has that in him."

That was something I could get excited about. "I see Benoit picking up the Vezina Trophy by the age of thirty."

I was confident that would be true. There was something about Benoit, a beauty in the way he connected with the ice in the same way as some of the best goalies in the game. All he needed was a good team in front of him, and he could be a hall of famer.

He could go all the way.

"Agreed." Coach pressed his fingers to the bridge of his nose. "Okay, this is no one's business but yours and Benoit's, so you're covered, and he is too. What I suggest is, you put this in writing, and Benoit does too, separately, and I'll respond officially on behalf of the team and college. There might not be anything endorsed in the NCAA guidelines, but I want to cross all my T's and dot all my I's. Two grown men have their own business to attend to, but we have to be sure, with you being in a position of influence, albeit in an unofficial capacity."

"I can always stand aside."

"I don't think that is something you have to do right now."

I pulled out the letter I'd already written and handed it over. The letter had been Downer's idea, my fellow coach thinking it a good idea to get those same I's and T's attended to that Coach had talked about.

"That's my letter. I'll let you go to Benoit direct, but right now, he wants what we have kept on the down low, wants to focus on his studying and his hockey."

Coach Quinton nodded. Then he crossed his arms over his chest and sat back in his seat. "Now, back to hockey. From a defense perspective, tell me what you think about Ryker Madsen. I'm having a hard time matching players to his speed for his line, and his wingers are vulnerable to other teams' D-men. I'd like to hear your thoughts on how we get him to slow down a little while not taking the shine off of what he can do."

Asking Ryker Madsen to slow down was like asking Downer not to keep reminding me of the embarrassing stories of when I was eighteen. Still, we managed to look at Ryker from a defense point of view, talked about Benoit, the D-corp, the forwards, and before I knew it, two hours had passed.

By the time I left the office, we'd hashed out a plan for Ryker, a solid defense plan for the team, and a promise I'd work with Downer on strategy. I still refused to be officially hired. I was there as a volunteer, and that was the way I wanted it to stay. I worked the same hours as Downer did, I was here at the rink more often than not, but that final tie was something to avoid.

I didn't know what I wanted to do next. I just knew it could possibly involve following Benoit to whatever city he ended up in.

I have it so bad.

I HAD to stop for a breather. If I'd still been an NHL player, I would've been working on my strength, not losing the edge, but I wasn't going back, and my muscles were telling me I was turning into a lazy ass.

If by lazy, I mean not training six hours a day and instead spending only an hour in the gym trying to do as much as I could with my leg still in a cast.

"Are you sure this is a Canadian tradition?" I was tired from crutching all the way to the top of this damn hill in Mineral Springs Park. Not that I could blame Benoit. After all, he'd asked me on more than one occasion if I was okay with this, but damn my hockey player's idiocy because I told him every time that I was fine. The cast was coming off this week, and then it was down to one hell of a lot of PT and repairing muscle wastage, but for now, I was on the crutches, with my decorated cast, wrapped up against the Owatonna cold, and celebrating Thanksgiving.

American Thanksgiving. Which to me is one whole day of food, drink, football, and vegging on the sofa nursing a beer.

But this was not what Thanksgiving was, it seemed, if you were in a relationship with an ornery Canadian who had decided that this American Thanksgiving would be done in a Canadian Thanksgiving style.

Which apparently meant a walk.

"I told you, we don't really do much celebrating. It's more about being thankful and getting out in the fresh air."

A walk. For fuck's sake. I grumbled and cursed at him, but secretly I enjoyed following him up the hill and staring at his ass for forty minutes.

"Yeah, well, next year we're doing it *my* way," I groused, and he sent me a look that spoke volumes.

Next year? We gonna be a couple next year? Will I be playing in a city a thousand miles from you? How will this work? The thoughts hung unspoken between us, and finally Benoit changed the subject altogether.

"This entire park was carved by melting glaciers," he announced, striding to the edge of the tree line and onto a small viewing platform.

"I did live here you know, but carry on." He shot me a grateful look.

"I love it up here. Scott and I would walk this way when we first came to Owatonna, but you know, studying, hockey, it's all too much now to fit in walking with no purpose and staring at a pretty view. Come see."

"I think the view from here is gorgeous," I teased as he turned to find me staring at him.

"Get your ass next to me," he ordered, and I crutched over to stand next to him and looked at the park. It was lovely up there, not Grand Canyon impressive or Pacific Ocean expansive. It didn't have tall monuments or anything super dramatic to break the wash of greens and blues, but what it did have was peace that I could get used to. Of course, having Benoit at my side was part of that peace.

"So, you want to hear the legend? About how the town got its name."

"As I said, I did live here, but you know what? I'd listen to you recite a shopping list," I teased, and we knocked elbows.

"Well, I think it's kind of cool. A tribal Chief had a daughter, Owatonna, but she was ill, like fading away kind of ill. So, he'd heard about some healing waters, and he moved his entire tribe to the site of the natural springs. Right there on the banks of Maple Creek." He pointed down at the ribbon of water that ran straight through the park. "They say that she drank from the springs and was all healed, and the legend is that her spirit is here on the banks of the river and welcomes travelers from all over."

"That's pretty much what I know as well."

"That's the legend, but actually Native Americans camped near the river, and they called it 'Ouitunya,' which means 'straight'. I kind of like the daughter story, though." He took my hand and laced our fingers, and I shuffled my foot a little to stand firm. "I'm sorry I made you listen to me tell all that, and come all the way up here."

"I'm enjoying you talking." We stood in silence a moment or so more, and I leaned on him more so I could stay standing. He took my weight and held me steady, and we kissed a few times, talking softly in between about the daughter and the river.

"I gave my letter to Coach Quinton," he announced on the way down. I was trying hard to stay upright, so didn't have a lot to say to him about that, but his tone implied he wanted to talk about it, and as soon as we were out of the cab and back in my house, I opened a conversation right up.

"Was it okay? Writing the letter I mean?"

He grinned that wide sexy grin of his that never failed to make me want to kiss him so damn bad. "It's all good." Then he leaned into me but nowhere near close enough to kiss, and I wasn't going to close the distance unless he wanted me to. I'd lost count of the days we'd been a thing, but every single hour with him, I wanted to touch him, kiss him, make him smile. I didn't want him to get bored with me or my kisses. It would've broken me if he ever turned to me and said he was done with me; that was how bad I had it. I changed the subject.

"So what's next today on this American-Thanksgiving-the-Canadian-way?"

"Ryker has this thing," Benoit murmured, "if you'd like to go. Would you? Everyone will be there. My friends, I mean, not his dad and Ten, because they're on the West Coast, but you'll meet Hayne and Scott, and I want you to meet Scott."

"I'd love to—"

"I get that it's hard, that you're a coach, and you know the guys in that capacity, well, Ryker at least, but Scott, I'm sure you've seen him out there, and they're my friends, and I want you to meet my friends, properly, off ice."

I summarized what he was asking. "You have an event that is something to do with Ryker, and everyone will be there, and you want me to go, or us, as a couple maybe."

He closed his eyes briefly. "You want to do that?"

"I said I'd love to."

"Really?"

"Why wouldn't I?" It seemed this wasn't a question I was getting an answer to, because Benoit leaped to his feet. He held out a hand to help me up, which I took because, sue me, I might have been able to stand on my own, but I'd have done anything to hold his hand. "Let's go."

"Now?" I looked down at my muddy jeans and thought about how my beanie had made my hair stick up like a porcupine. Not to mention I hadn't shaved. "Can I just have an hour to make myself look…"

He knocked shoulders with me. "An hour in the shower sounds good." He walked away toward the bathroom and glanced over his shoulder at me. "I'll wrap your leg," he said with a wink.

I'd never moved from my kitchen to the bathroom as fast as I did, losing the crutches and hobbling. Benoit and water, maybe a blow job? Yep, I was all over that. I wrapped my cast in a haphazard fashion and climbed in. When he went to his knees, staring up at me, his eyes wide with passion and his lips wrapped around my cock, I didn't close my eyes but watched every wet, erotic, moment, his hands on my hips helping to hold me steady. I pushed him away at the last moment, wanting to see myself coming over his dark skin, and I couldn't help the words that slipped out, even with how hard I'd been trying to wait.

"I love you," I said, and then I closed my eyes because it was too early, and he'd just stare at me as if I was fucking mad.

Only he didn't.

He stood, pressed his weight into me, slotting his hard cock against my thigh and sliding it in the tight space between us, and he stared at me, didn't take his eyes off me, groaning at his release, kissing me hard, and pulling back a little.

"Well, shit," he said, "I love you, too."

"Too fast for you?" I asked because he needed to know that I was worried.

But he smiled at me, kissed me, and we stood under the warm water.

"When you know, you know."

NINE

Benoit

I WAS MORE THAN A LITTLE NERVOUS ABOUT BRINGING
Ethan to the house. It was one of the heaviest things that
I'd been carrying around. Ethan and my friends, hockey,
school, and the arrival of another one of those pink
envelopes yesterday. I'd found it propped up inside my
cubicle in the Eagles dressing room, resting inside a spare
helmet, inked-on eyes staring at me from within the
confines of my headgear. It scared the living shit out of
me. Even with a room full of burly men, I felt exposed,
alone, and terrified.

I didn't open it. I threw it into my bag, hiding it among
papers and notes, unsure how to deal with the situation.
Was it someone on the team? It had to be, right? Who else
had access to my stuff, to this area, unless it was another
player? But the notes felt personal. Really personal. As if
this sick person and I had history. But that was impossible.
I hadn't dated anyone on the team or any other sports team
on campus. A couple of girls here and there, but women
weren't allowed in the locker room so…

Just when I thought I'd gotten past the worst stuff, this started. Inhaling deeply, I pushed the worry into a dark place, as I had all the notes, and focused on the current worry, which was Ethan and my housemates.

Not that I thought he'd embarrass me or anything like that. It was more how Ryker, Scott, and Hayne would react to him and me as a couple.

"Are we going in anytime soon?" Ethan asked, his words clouds of steam that blew away on a crisp Minnesota breeze. "Not that I dislike admiring doors. This one is a particular beauty, late nineteen eighties if I'm not mistaken. Eggshell-white with a lovely set of brass hinges and—"

"Okay, smartass, I get it," I said with an eye roll, then threw the door open. He maneuvered his way through the door, I followed, and we both sighed at the smell of roast turkey.

"This is going to be so good." Ethan grinned as we peeled off our coats and boots. "Did I mention that I hold the Owatonna County Fair record for pie eating?"

"You did not mention that," I said, motioning him toward the kitchen at the back of the house. There was a lot we didn't know about each other. Had we rushed into saying that L-word too quickly? Maybe we should have waited? Perhaps it would set us up for failure, confessing such deep emotions when we'd only been together such a short time?

"Hey, it's all going to be okay," Ethan whispered before we arrived in the kitchen.

"Sure, yeah, I know."

And it was. Ryker, Scott, and Hayne welcomed Ethan into the fold as if he'd always been one of the guys. There was no weird "God he is so old" comments or looks as we sat around the table, stuffing ourselves on turkey, mashed potatoes, corn, dressing, and cranberry sauce. Part of the reason Ethan fit in so well, I felt, was that he never tried to be the adult in the group. He melded perfectly into the mindset of college students. Not sure if that was a good thing or not, but his laid-back, corny joking eased my worries. By the time we had finished the main course, Ethan had everyone laughing over some stupid story about a plane ride with a particularly gassy Boston goalie.

"I'm not kidding. By the time the plane landed in Tampa, everyone was in the back of the jet besides our tender, who vowed he would eat nothing but beans from that day forward just to ensure his flights were quiet," Ethan said, then chuckled.

"No, let us clean up," Scott said when Hayne rose and started picking up dirty plates.

Ryker and I nodded. "You sit. We'll bring out dessert and coffee," I told Ethan. He winked at me as I stood. Hands full of plates, I followed Ryker into the kitchen. "Hayne really cooks well," I said, placing the dishes into the new dishwasher.

"He said his Mimi sent him all her recipes. Shame his mom and she were both sick with the flu. I bet he misses them," Ryker said while scraping leftover corn into a smaller bowl.

"Yeah, I bet he does. Listen, I just wanted to thank you." Ryker glanced over at me. "For being cool about Ethan and me. I know he's older and all."

"Dude, really? Like I'm going to give you shit over dating an older man? Hello! Have you ever met my two dads?" Ryker flicked a kernel of corn at me. I swatted it aside. It hit Scott on the nose as he walked in with a platter of half-eaten turkey.

"Assholes," Scott mumbled, just as someone hammered on the door.

"I'll get it!" I yelled, dancing around Scott with grace and slick dance floor moves that put the two losers in the kitchen to shame. I jogged to the door, snickering over the corn-to-nose incident, and yanked it open. There on the step was Jacob, his eyes glowing, his nose red, and his hands balancing a pie.

I gaped at him for a second. "Ryker didn't say you were coming."

"He doesn't know. Here." He handed me the pie and snuck inside, his finger over his pursed lips. I nodded, closed the door with my foot, and followed him into the kitchen.

"Some dude is here with a pie for dessert," I shouted over Jacob's shoulder. Ryker turned his head, and his mouth fell open. Good thing I now held the pie because Ryker launched himself at Jacob. The big man caught his boyfriend with a grunt, hands under Ryker's ass, and kissed him for so long I began to wonder if they were going to get down to it right here next to the pie.

"What are you doing here?" Ryker gasped, sliding his hands over Jacob's pink cheeks, his eyes more than a little dewy. "You said maybe Christmas."

"Yeah, I kind of lied. My uncle is here from Montana, and he's going to help with the chores, so Dad gave me an advance on my wages, and Mom gave me a pie, and they told me to get my ass to Owatonna. If you don't want me underfoot for a few days, I can go back home."

"Like hell!" Ryker pulled his mouth back to his.

"So yeah, why don't we serve the pie and coffee, Scott?" I asked, slipping around the two men devouring each other.

"Right, yep, coffee and pie." Scott nudged me in the side. Then we left the reunited lovers in the kitchen.

"Ryker's boyfriend showed up and surprised him," I said as we sat down. Hayne grinned widely. "We might not see them for dessert, but hey, we have pie made by a mom!"

Ethan made yummy noises and ate four slices of Mrs. Benson's apple pie. I caught sight of Ryker and Jacob sneaking up the stairs as I was sipping my coffee. I had keen goalie vision. It was hard to slip something past me. We didn't see either of them until the following morning. Which was fine because that was when my roommates snuck a peek at me and Ethan. No point sending him home now that the guys knew about—and were cool—with us. Besides, he had pie belly and needed someone to rub his distended stomach until he fell asleep. The things we do for love…

WE HAD a game the following Saturday in Michigan. I kissed Ethan goodbye at home, wishing he could travel along, but he was really only a volunteer and it wasn't appropriate. Also, as he pointed out, it was good to spend time apart. He'd be there when I got back, waiting, cast-free as he was heading in this morning to have it removed.

The team lucked out, and we jumped a charter flight, making what would have been a nearly thirteen-hour road trip on a bus a short ninety or so minutes. The Greater

Michigan University campus was about forty minutes outside of Detroit, a town that took its hockey seriously. And the GMU Moose were the favorite sons of the state. They'd been ripping up their opponents. We had a good chance of slowing them down, as we had two things they didn't—Ryker Madsen and me.

I know that was cocky, and my folks would've turned inside out if they'd heard me talking like that, but an athlete had to have confidence. And now that things in my personal life were settled, my focus had zeroed back in on hockey. Ethan understood. He'd lived his ice hockey dream. Now it was my turn, and he supported me wholly. I refused to dwell on the where and what of what would happen after I graduated, or those creepy notes. Hopefully, I'd be living in Edmonton with Ethan, and my secret stalker would have moved on to someone else, since I wouldn't be around anymore. Laying low was paying off. Just had to keep my head down.

Right now, though, this game and this ice was my main focus. Michigan had crappy water. It was impure and made flaky ice that didn't work well. I tended to my crease, sprinkling droplets of pure Canadian water on the blue ice, and then working it into a fine little frozen wall that would, I hoped, help deflect a puck. I tapped the pipes when I was done, looking up to find one of the Moose players staring at me oddly.

I threw my hand in the air, and he skated off, shaking his head. His last name was Devon. When we were finished with our warm-up, I skated over, handed our equipment manager my tiny squirt bottle of water from home, and sat on the boards, resting, sipping water, readying myself for the game. After a moment or two of waiting for the officials to join us, I took my mask from Ryker, patted the Eagle on the side, and skated to my net. Yes, the ice was good now, firmer, not flaky like before. This game would be ours. I felt it in my bones.

The first period was slow, few shots on goal for either side. The teams were feeling each other out, the coaching staff adjusting here and there as the lines began to show strengths and weaknesses. There were perhaps three or so minutes left. I was resting a bit in my stance, bent over, crossbar on my back, eyes on the action down at the Moose end of the ice, when one of the players in red stole the puck from our fourth line. He was fast, his gaze familiar as he streaked at me. Devon. His first name might have been David, but I wasn't sure. His puck handling was fair, but he telegraphed his moves. I saw him shift left, and settled back on my skates, easily catching the weak shot from point. He lost his edge on the crappy ice and careened into me, knocking me off my skates and dislodging the net. It was a meager collision, nothing really, and my teammates hustled up as they always do when a player makes contact with a goalie.

There were some words exchanged, what, I couldn't hear as the linesman was shouting at the guys to stop shoving. Ryker, who had just hit the ice after the breakaway, grabbed Devon, who was now on his feet, and threw a punch that leveled the guy. I sat there, stunned, puck in my catcher mitt, as several shades of madness erupted right in my crease. Ryker was off his mind with rage. It took two players and a ref to tug him off Devon, and even when they'd been separated, they kept jawing at each other. I got up and shouted at my teammates to find out what had been said.

"You know what I called you!" Devon roared at me adding the N-word and cursing. I blinked, salty sweat in my eyes, unsure if what I had heard was what I had heard. "I said to get off me you dirty—" Ryker went at Devon again, hitting him in the back of the head with a closed fist that put the man down face-first on the ice.

The hometown fans were not happy. And then the chant began. The same slur about the color of my skin that had been slung at me by Devon was now being repeated by the fans. Just a few, not the whole crowd, but enough that the message was clearly delivered. My teammates all stared at me, horror and anger on their faces.

"Fuck them," I said as Ryker was led off the ice, bruised and bloody knuckles, his face contorted with white-hot ire, his upper lip busted from a stick or an elbow delivered in the scrum. "Let's play hockey."

I got some back slaps and a few helmet rubs. The chanting eased off. I hoped that was due to security removing the racist fans from their seats.

"Hey, man, we're not all like Devon," Chris Milliken, the Moose captain, told me after making a point to skate over amid all the carnage. He offered me his hand. I shook off my blocker and took his hand. People applauded. Things returned to normal on the ice, and we wrapped up the final minutes with a shaky sort of subdued cloud hanging over us.

I left the ice feeling unsure of myself and the world I was moving in. I'd faced racism before, of course, being one of a handful of black players in a predominately white man's game, but I'd *never* been chanted at like that. It was different to hear one man toss something vile at you; a group yelling racist slurs was something else. It was frightening.

"Hey, hey, you okay?" Ryker asked, meeting me at the door of the locker room, his upper lip cut and seeping blood around the quick four stitches he'd just gotten.

"I'm better than you," I replied, hoping to sound nonchalant. I must've failed. Several of the Eagles gathered around me, roasting Devon verbally, saying they all had his number and were going to make sure the dirty bastard felt every check.

I nodded, smiled, tried to play it off as no big thing, but it *had* been. It had scared me, hearing that word bouncing off the girders, seeing the fans by the glass with clear hatred in their eyes. Yeah, that shit had unnerved me.

I glanced back when someone called my name. Coach motioned for me to follow him, so I pushed to my skates, gave Ryker a shrug, and plodded along after my head coach.

We went only as far as the skate-sharpening room when he turned to me. "I feel as if I need to apologize for the whole hockey community," Coach said, twisting his hands as he searched my face for clues to where I was. "That was uncalled-for behavior. I want you to know that I've already filed a grievance against Devon and that the fans who were being so disgusting have been ejected from the arena. I wish I could promise you that they'd been removed from the campus, but some of them are students, I'm sure. Please be aware of that when you leave the rink."

"Okay, I will be." What more could I say? Now I had to look over my shoulder walking from the rink to the bus?

When would people just stop with the hating of others?

"Thanks, Coach."

"You good?"

"Yeah, I'm good. Ready to play."

"Okay, good." He patted my well-padded shoulder. "You know I'm normally not a fan of these things, but I thought you might want to take this call. Make it short."

He handed me his cell phone and walked back to the away locker room, presumably to talk to the team about the ugliness that had taken place. I turned from the hall, burrowing into a small nook that held a water cooler, and placed the phone to my ear.

"Son, are you okay?" Dad asked, his voice thick with emotion.

"You were watching on the streaming app?" I asked, my shoulders humped, my back and neck slick with sweat. Now I wanted to cry, and a stray tear slipped free before I could dash it away with the sleeve of my sweater.

"Yeah, I was watching. I am so sorry, Benoit. So horribly sorry. I can fly out. Would you like that?"

I drew in a shaky breath. "No, it's cool. I'm fine. It's just…" I blew out a breath. "I just don't get it, you know? What difference does the color of my skin make?"

"None, my son, none at all. We love you. You go out there, and you show them just how fine a job you can do in that crease."

"I will, Dad, I promise. I miss you. Can't wait for Christmas. I think I might be asking someone to come home with me if that's okay?"

"Well, of course it is, Benoit."

"It's a man."

"Then we'll make sure we put shaving cream in the

guest bathroom instead of those bath bomb glittery things your sister is so fond of."

I kind of wept hard then, just for a few seconds, and then sucked all the love and hurt and confusion back inside. How lucky was I to have a family this amazing? Damn lucky.

"You okay, son?"

"Yeah, I'm… phew, yep. I'm good. Tell Mom not to be upset about it. Some people are just stupid dumb."

"Son, you know your mother. She's ready to fly to Michigan and start kicking ass and taking names," Dad replied, then laughed along with me. "Now you go out there, and you stand on your head."

"I will, I promise. Thanks, Dad. I love you. See you over Christmas."

"We love you too, son, and we are so proud. Now go give them hell."

I hung up, and then I went back on the ice and showed the Moose and all their fans just what I could do in net. Which was stop forty out of forty shots and give the Eagles a win.

WHEN WE ARRIVED BACK in Minnesota, the airport was snowy and the wind was blowing fat flakes around in whirling funnels of snow and dust. Ethan was there, waiting, and I couldn't get into his arms quickly enough. He held me tight—too tight to be honest—but I didn't try to break free. I needed his arms around me like I needed my next breath.

"I love you more than pie," he whispered in my ear. A

wobbly barking laugh escaped me, and I pressed a kiss to his neck. His skin was warm and soft right under his ear.

"That's a lot of love right there," I murmured beside his ear, my teammates rolling past us, not a one saying a word about two men hugging it out in public.

"Damn straight." He gave me a final cinch, then released me, taking my bag from my shoulder and staring into my soul. "My place, your place, or the pie place?"

"There's a pie place?"

"Well, it's not a pie place; it's a cupcake place, which is sort of as good as pie, but not really. Want to grab some cupcakes? We can lie around in bed, get all crumby and frosted up, and use our tongues to clean each other off." He waggled a brow. I snorted. "That a yes?"

"Yes, it's a yes."

"I knew I loved you for a reason." He leaned on his new cane, and we slowly left the terminal, his fingers linked with mine for all the travelers and workers to see. We drove home, touching lightly and avoiding the nastiness the world had dumped on me, stopping only for a run into the cupcake shop, then to his place, where we locked the doors on the outside world and carried those dozen delights to his bedroom.

"You do know that I was joking about the sexy cupcake times, right?"

I took the box from him, placed it on the bed, and began peeling his clothing off, one article at a time.

"I joke a lot, like when I'm nervous or unsure of how to handle a certain situation."

I pulled his shirt over his head, dropped it to the floor, then I snapped his belt free from the loops, whipped it over my shoulder, and tugged down his fly after freeing the snap holding his jeans shut.

"I know you just suffered something really traumatic, and I'm not sure if sexing it up is the best thing to do."

"What would you rather I do? Sit down and cry? Shake my fist at the bigotry of the world? Slam my head against the wall at the injustice of being judged for my skin color or my sexual preferences?"

"I, uhm, I don't know. I'm just… sorry."

And I knew he was. I could see it in his gaze. "Look, this here, what we have, this is pure love. It's the two of us about to be one. No outside crap, no labels, just two souls seeking to be close, to feel one another, to pleasure one another. This is the most right thing in the world."

He inhaled slowly, through his nose, and cupped my face between his hands. "Damn, you are something else." He put his mouth over mine, the kiss gentle at first, but growing into something more as we went to the bed, his hands moving over me, freeing me of my shirt and pants, my socks and underwear, as I worked on his few remaining bits of clothing. He sat on the edge of the mattress, hands on my bare ass, and pulled me to him. "Don't hate me if you end up picking sprinkles out of delicate places tomorrow during class."

That made me laugh. He nipped at my chest, a nipple, my navel, and then he took me into his mouth. His tongue rolled over my cockhead; my fingers dug into his shoulders. He licked and lapped, sucking hard, then pulling off until I gave him a shove that sent him sprawling back onto the mattress.

I climbed over him, one leg settling by his hip, then the other, my lips tracing patterns over his flesh, tasting as much as I could before I was once again licking into his mouth.

"Give me that," he growled when I reached for the cupcakes. I shook my head, holding the box upward, away from him. A wicked smile played on his lips. With a poke to my ribs, the box tumbled to the bed. We both pounced on it, laughing like idiots. The cupcakes didn't fare well. I'd had this erotic imagery of using a finger to paint icing designs on his fair skin. Instead, we both ended up with mangled bits of cake and rainbow-toned frosting all over us, the cover, and the nightstand. Even the lampshade had purple icing on it, but that was okay. It was *all* okay. The blue icing on the box of condoms, the pink icing on the tube of lubricant, and the yellow icing worked into the fine hairs of his chest.

"Ben, babe, you sure?" He sounded winded, but it was passion pulling the air from his lungs as I eased myself down on him, even the condom stretched tightly over his dick had green icing fingerprints all over it. The stretch was intense, painful yes, but only for a moment until my body relaxed around him. "Christ…"

"Sure, yeah, so sure," I whispered, settling downward inch by inch until he was buried in my ass. My fingers, coated with indigo frosting and sugary sprinkles, dug into his pectorals, my hips rolling. "God, so good. Sweet."

"Mm, so sweet." He peeled my hand from his chest and led my fingers to his mouth. His pupils were fat and black, his whiskery cheeks and eyebrows layered with white cake crumbs and orange icing. As I rocked back and forth, he sucked my fingers clean, one by one, both hands, and then pulled me down, hand to my nape, and began lapping at the powdered sugar and raspberry jam crusted on my throat and shoulder. "When you're close, come on my chest. I want to taste it all. The cake, the jelly, the frosting, you. I want to take all of you into me."

"Shit yes, yes, I will," I gasped, kissing his mouth wildly, moving faster and harder, his cock pegging my prostate with each thrust. "I want you to come on yourself too. I want to taste us both, all of it... damn, I'm really close."

He grabbed my ass, lifting me, trying to slow things, but I was too far gone for that. I wiggled free, dropping onto his cock with force. He groaned, I yelped, and I shot hard, ribboning his chest.

"Up, fuck, get up," he snarled, bucking until his dick popped free. I was humped over him, jerking my dick when he came, the condom tossed to the floor. His fingers fumbled with mine, lining up our pricks and we worked ourselves off together. When the first pulses subsided, I stretched out over him, smearing the icing and jimmies, cake and jam, semen and sweat, between our chests. He wanted that first taste, so I shimmied upward, trembling still as he lapped at my chest and belly, his moans of pleasure pulling another spurt of cum from me.

"My turn," I huffed, out of breath but still insanely turned on. I buried my face in his belly, rubbing on him like a cat. Then I licked his navel, tonguing the divot clean of pure white icing. Down to his cock I went, working the spunk into the jam, then taking his cock down my throat. His ass left the bed. I choked and purred, reveling in the mixture of sweet and salty as it coated my tongue.

"Come here... up here," he said, using his fingers in my sticky hair to lead my lips back to his. "I love you, every single inch of you. Every part of you, every damn thing about you." The kiss was long, sweet, sinful, tender, magnificent. Everything we were, Ethan and Benoit, was in that kiss. I never wanted it to stop. Ever. There was no older man and younger man, no black or white, no American and Canadian. There was just us, and we were so crazy mad in love it made me feel that anything and everything was possible.

TEN

Ethan

I'D LOST MY DINING ROOM COMPLETELY.

Not that I actually used the huge oak table or the twelve chairs that surrounded it. I'd never lit the candles that stood in the center of it, and the paintings on the wall were generic and left over from the house being dressed for rental. In fact, before Benoit had visited the house, I hadn't stepped inside the room since I'd looked around that first day. But this was Benoit's spot now on the odd nights he stayed over. The table was spread with textbooks, hockey notes, large sheets of paper with complicated plans, and piles of note books, along with scattered pens and at least four rulers. What he needed four rulers for I didn't know, but it was something I teased him about, and it never failed to make him smile.

I loved it when Benoit smiled.

He'd stayed over last night, and we'd woken up this lazy Sunday morning, made long slow love, and then after a breakfast of pancakes and eggs, he'd dressed in sweats and an Eagles T-shirt, then taken up his usual position at the table. He was muttering to himself as he furiously scribbled on paper, and I placed the coffee next to him and then pressed a kiss to his neck. He at least stopped muttering, but not before he'd jumped in surprise.

"Sorry," I immediately apologized, understanding he'd been deep in thought. I'd never attended college and had left school as soon as I could. After being drafted, that had been me and professional hockey in an intimate fulfilling relationship for fourteen years. I had no concept of the kind of pressure Benoit and his friends must've been under trying to balance hockey and studying. Ben sighed heavily and turned in his chair, glancing up at me.

"No, I'm sorry, I'm just tense," he explained and then pursed his lips for a kiss, which I was more than happy to give him.

"What is it that has you so tense?" I looked over his shoulder at the scribbles in a notebook he had open next to an iPad. "The development of critical thinking as the primary goal of educational process," I read the title and scanned the headings under it. "You have to do that?"

"Two thousand words, by Thursday," he said with another full-body sigh.

"How many words do you have so far?" Maybe that wasn't a good question to ask, because he frowned and then buried his head on his crossed arms.

"Twelve. I have twelve words."

Okay, that didn't sound good, but I could be the supportive partner. "Twelve. "Twelve is better than nothing."

"Count the words in the title."

"Huh?"

"Count them."

I dutifully counted each word. "Twelve."

"Yeah, see?"

"The title is your twelve words?"

"Only one thousand, nine hundred and eighty-eight to go," he said.

I bit back the snort of laughter because this shit was serious and meant something to Benoit, but the hangdog expression on his face made me smirk just a little. "I'll leave you to it," I said and began to back out of the room.

"You have to help me. Tell me what your opinion is of critical thinking and whether it's the primary goal of education."

I slowed my roll, but only enough to fake staying, and then I darted out of the room. "Sorry, I need to make calls," I said over my shoulder, and he snorted a laugh at me. At least my presence in the room had meant something to him. Anyway, I wasn't lying. I had a call to return from Brady Rowe, who'd left a garbled message about retirement and players and something else I couldn't make out. Settled with my coffee, I returned his call and put him on speaker phone so I could sit on the heated patio and stare out over the extensive yard and lawn beyond.

"Seriously? You're not coming back to the team, and I have to hear it from Ten?" Brady snapped as soon as he answered.

"Hello to you too," I deadpanned.

"Don't fuck with me, Ethan. Jared's kid, Ryker told Ten that you're really retiring. I thought you were in negotiations with Boston after you came back on IR. Shit, did they not offer you anything?"

"No, and that's okay. You know I'm thirty-two, Brady. I'm tired." I'd never have admitted that to any other player, but Brady was my closest friend, someone I'd taken under my wing when he'd come to the team, even knowing one day he'd be captain and wouldn't need me. I liked to think he relied on my common sense. I relied on his skill as captain, and he was one of the guys I'd miss most.

He was still huffing. "Look, I'll talk to management, force them to offer you another year. You know they'll listen to me."

I laughed because this was the perfect moment for me to ride his ass about his gifted little brother. "Brady, you always were too fond of your imagined power. Now, if your name was *Tennant* Rowe, then maybe management would give in to blackmail."

"Fuck you," Brady said, but it wasn't said with any heat, and he laughed as he spoke. The entire Boston team rode him for being the older brother to the newest, brightest hockey phenom, and he'd gotten used to it. But he soon grew serious as he circled back to me retiring. "Seriously, Ethan, this is shit. Why won't Boston give you another year? I don't get it. You're the best D-man on the team."

"I used to be, but I'm slower now, and you need new blood."

Brady was silent for a while, and I could imagine his thoughts: he was twenty-eight, right at the peak of his skills, the captain of an original six team, but even his days were numbered. I thought maybe losing me, the first of his closest friends, would be a stark wakeup call about the longevity of a playing career. There were only a few players who carried on into their thirties, a couple in their forties, goalies, only one or two players, but the average

age of forwards and defensemen retiring from hockey was thirty or thereabouts. At thirty-two, I was bucking the trend. "You're really doing this? You're not even trying for another team? You're done?"

"I wasn't. I mean, my agent had feelers out, even got me a possible on the West Coast, but then I came home, and then my leg, and now…"

"What?"

I glanced at the shut door to the dining room and couldn't find the words at first. My chest was tight with emotion, and the weight of the decisions I needed to make was a heavy one. I didn't need the money, and I could to buy a house in whatever city I ended up in. But hockey had defined me for so long, and when my leg was healed, then there was no reason not to play.

"I've got time," I began. I knew that this meant nothing to Brady right now, although it would when he faced his own retirement. Brady was a bossy, unrelenting team player, and I knew damn well he'd make an excellent coach, with the famous Rowe hockey-vision. His path was clearer than mine. Or at least it had been clearer until I'd met Benoit and abruptly knew exactly what I wanted, which was to be wherever he was. "I want a place or person to call home and the chance to think about what to do next, and in a month I might decide to go to Europe and play there or coach or set up a hockey school or become an astronaut. I never gave a second thought to anything besides hockey, and it feels… right, to be doing this now. You get that?"

Brady sighed, just as noisily as Benoit had done over his studies. "I always imagined you'd leave when I did.

Hell, we have this kid, Austin. He moved up from the Bears, and he's working your D-pair."

"I know. I've seen him. He's good."

"He's nineteen, for fuck's sake."

It sounded to me like Brady was feeling his age the same as I was. "You'll show him what you need from him. He's an asset that you can polish."

"Fuck," Brady snapped with feeling, "this feels like I'm a teenager who's just lost his first love."

"I knew you wanted my ass, really."

"Fuck you, Ethan, for making me feel so shit. I miss your ugly face."

"I love you too." I smirked. Then it hit me this was my best friend talking, and I had something I really wanted to share with him. I toed the door of the sunroom shut. "So I met someone," I began. Brady and I didn't do this personal stuff normally, or at least not to this depth, but I wanted to run down the street shouting about Benoit, and I couldn't, so Brady was the next best thing. "He's a senior at college, a goalie. His name's Benoit."

Silence. So much silence that I leaned over to check we were still connected.

Finally Brady spoke. "A senior, so that makes him what, twenty-two?"

I bristled a little at the tone of Brady's voice. "Yeah." *Here comes the criticism or the what-ifs.*

"Well, it works for Mads and Ten." I could hear the shrug from here. "He make you happy?"

"Yeah."

"Look, don't disconnect me, but I owe you my honesty here. Is he the reason you're giving it all up?"

The implication I was giving something up was misplaced. I wasn't giving anything up at all. I was just looking to move forward with a man I loved. How did I explain that, though? I couldn't expect Brady to understand.

"Not directly, no," I gave the simple answer, "but he is part of the reason I can look to the future with so much expectation and positivity. You get that, right?"

More silence. Then Brady snorted a laugh. "Bring him to a game. I want to meet this guy. Give me a heads-up, and we'll arrange something."

With that call done, I had one more to make. My agent had texted me twice this morning, and a hundred times over the past few weeks with various possible lucrative roles for an aging player. Eli wasn't taking no for an answer, and I owed him the honesty of my decision. He answered on the first ring.

"Ethan, I was just about to call you. Vancouver came through with a one-year offer, depending on physical assessment, two way to—"

"Eli, stop. I want you to stop. I'm making my retirement official." I waited for the explosion, but instead, Eli was very calm when he answered.

"Is that your final answer?"

I thought about making a joke about phoning a friend but wondered if that cultural reference would open him to thinking I wasn't serious.

"Absolutely. Check your inbox. I made it official this morning." He didn't have to know that pressing send had been the easiest thing I'd ever done and also one of the hardest. Everything was so utterly final but was filled with possibilities.

"What will you do?" Eli asked, and I didn't have an answer.

"Volunteer some more, and take a *really* long holiday."

"I can't say I'm shocked. I've been expecting this, and you'll be missed. It's been a good run, hasn't it?"

Fourteen years, two teams, cups, awards, and no long-lasting injuries. Yeah, things had been very good.

"Yeah."

"Okay then." He was suddenly less emotional and more efficient. "I'll tie up the loose ends, get a press release issued," he said, and then with the formalities done, I only had one more thing to say.

"Thank you, Eli, again, for everything."

"You're welcome. It's been a ride."

When all that was done, I called Mom and Dad, but they'd already known most of it. I was looking forward to them meeting Benoit, and they promised they'd visit when they could. I fired emails to extended family, friends, explained what was happening and to expect a press release, and then I headed straight back to the dining room because right now, I needed to see Benoit. Just be near him while not interrupting him studying. I picked up more coffee and a supply of his favorite cookies and headed in, standing in the doorway for the longest time and staring at the man who'd stolen my heart. He was so focused I didn't think he even knew I was there, but he did glance up and smile at me when I sat on the corner next to him.

"Give me five," he said abstractedly, and worrying at his lower lip with his teeth, he typed furiously on the small battered keyboard. I could get him a new one and a better iPad. I could give him anything he wanted, and the thought made me smile. I sipped coffee and nibbled at triple chocolate goodness, idly scanning the books in front of me, opening one and closing it when I read a few paragraphs of notes on dynamism, which was apparently a thing in the classroom. I moved the pile away from my mug, just in case of spills, and pieces of paper came loose, some pink envelopes with black hearts inked on them among the usual junk. I quickly pushed them back where they'd come from, and then a word in a huge font jumped out at me. I eased the paper loose and read the message on it.

I SAW U KISSING HIM, *and I don't like it. How can U be the best if U waste time with him? U mine, baby. I'll destroy him before I let him ruin what we want. Love U. ALWAYS.*

I READ IT AGAIN, turned the page over, checking for more, like a name or some idea of who might have sent it, but it was generic paper with no signature.

"What is this? Some kind of joke from one of the team?" I thought maybe it was a joke, and I wasn't expecting the reaction I got from Benoit, who snatched it off of me with a curse and thrust it into his laptop bag.

"It's nothing," he snapped and zipped the bag as if a zipper would stop me from getting that piece of paper back out if I wanted. I was an NHL defenseman, and I knew how to get the puck off of the most tenacious of players; a bag would be nothing.

"Benoit?"

He dipped his head and began to collect up his things. "That's my private shit."

I attempted to defuse the situation with humor. "You shouldn't have left it on the table."

He looked up at me. "I didn't. I hid it in the—"

I wasn't calm about this at all. "What? You hid it? From me?"

"I have my own life, and it's nothing. I'm ignoring them."

I pushed my half-full mug aside carefully and laid my hands on the table. "'Them'? You're ignoring *them*. You've received other notes like this? Start talking, Benoit."

He stood, giving up on being organized and unzipped his bag, pushing things inside.

"Don't talk to me as if I was a kid!" he shouted.

I sat back in my seat in shock. I could play this two ways. I could pin him down and make him tell me, or I could try and stay reasonable. For some reason, Benoit was hiding notes that were possibly as creepy as that one, and his defensiveness had me on edge.

"I'm not," I said calmly. "I'm talking to you as your lover." I didn't move an inch as he scooped the last notebook up, then corralled the rulers and shoved them in with so much force that one of them snapped. He was angry, seemed as though he wanted to lash out, and then as suddenly as his temper had flared, it subsided, and he slumped back in his chair as if his strings had been cut. He seemed defeated, unsure, devastated.

"I don't know where to start." His tone was so soft I had to strain to hear.

"Start from the beginning," I said and reached out to take a hand. "What is this all about?"

"Ethan, please…"

I laced our fingers and squeezed. "I love you, Benoit. I'm not going anywhere. Now, talk to me."

ELEVEN

Benoit

I STARED AT OUR INTERTWINED FINGERS, LYING OVER MY essay and the other scattered bits of paper, among the notes and scribbles, that latest note.

"Ben, talk to me…"

I looked up from our hands to his worried eyes. "I don't want you to worry. I don't want anyone to worry, my parents, my sister. They all have enough to fret over. I refuse to add to that. It's nothing…"

He squeezed my fingers lightly, his gaze growing serious. "That kind of thing is not *nothing*, Ben. That's a threat."

"It's someone pranking me, trying to throw me off my game, make me nervous." I glanced at the paper I should've been working on. I was falling behind. Life was piling up. The pressure was growing weightier with each passing day.

"Hey, look at me." I did as he asked. "Do you think this is related to that incident in Michigan?"

"I don't think so," I whispered as if speaking about this out loud would bring the media to his door. "Some of those people were angry, really angry, but the notes have been coming since before that Michigan crap."

His eyes flared. "There's more than one of these?" I nodded. He rocketed to his feet, shoving his hands through his hair. "How many? When did it start? Where are they all?"

"I put the other ones away."

"What? Where?"

"In our room, in my draw. Ethan, please don't freak out. This is just some stupid prank." I slapped the threatening note. He limped from one end of the table, then back, his anger and concern thick on the air.

"You're not that stupid. Don't sit there and try to feed me bullshit. I can see the fear in your eyes. You know this is way more than some prank by a fellow student or someone from an opposing team trying to mess with your head." He grabbed the note with the bold, black lettering and shook it at me. "This is a threat. This is someone confessing that they've been following you, stalking you! This is proof that some sick bastard is out there watching us. Do not try to fob this off as a joke. You need to go to the cops."

"No!" I slapped the note out of his hand, grabbed it before it hit the table, and crammed it into my backpack. "I'm not going to the cops. That's all I need, a bunch of cops digging into my past, asking questions, making statements to the press. You think Edmonton wants a player with that kind of baggage? They've still not commented on that racial shit in Michigan other than the standard statement."

They'd condemned divisive speech and expressed the sentiment that players of all races and sexual orientation were welcome in their organization. They just hadn't specifically referenced me.

"They supported you openly, Ben. What did you want them to do? Go slap the shit out of some drunk college kids?" He made another pass around the table, his limp growing worse with each step.

"Why don't you sit down?" I asked, worried about him, his leg, the stress in the air, and the fact that someone was, as he had said, watching me. Watching us. Maybe they were outside the window right now. My skin grew clammy and cold. "Please, sit down and stop yelling."

"Sorry, sorry, I'm just…" He exhaled, scrubbed his face with his hands, and then fell back into the chair beside me. "Ben, this is serious. You need to give those notes to the police."

I shook my head strongly. "No, I can't have anything else fall on me, Ethan. There are still reporters pestering me for an interview about the race troubles."

"If you'd talk to them, just one of them, they'd stop hounding you."

Again, I shook my head. He'd been saying that since that horrible night. Advising me to speak out and call it out. Tell the world what I thought, how I felt, and how that kind of bigotry hurt everyone, not just the players of color.

"I want it to die down. I need to be picked for the team, come fall. My family need that money."

"I'll give you money."

I scowled. That was yet another topic of heated discussion. My parents' financial issues. If we'd bickered about him giving me money to send to them once, we'd bickered a thousand times over it. My answer was always the same. No. I was the son. It was up to me to take care of my parents and sister now. Me. Not my boyfriend. Not the world. Not the government. Me.

"No, you won't." I stood, grabbed my papers, and began filling my backpack. "I'm not talking about this anymore, any of it. No," I snapped when he began to speak. "I'm done with it. I cannot be seen as disruptive to my future team. Nothing else matters but me making the cut in the fall. And all this other shit that's fucking with my head has to be forgotten. The press, the Michigan shit, the notes…"

"Me?"

"If you don't get off my fucking back… maybe!" Ethan said nothing as I shoved my arms into my coat and stalked out into the bitter cold of a bleak December day. Christmas was two weeks away. Ho-ho-ho. The house across the street was decorated already. Lights on the windows, a Santa and sleigh in the yard, and a big old green wreath on the door. My mother always had a live wreath and tree. Their house probably smelled like pine and cookies. She'd be baking nonstop from here on out, filling boxes with cookies for me to bring back to Minnesota. She worked so hard. Now she had to work even harder because Dad's condition wasn't improving, and my sister was applying to universities throughout Canada and the States. They never talked about the strain, but it had to be there. Mom needed me to succeed. I couldn't let stupid shit get in the way. I had to stay focused, or my whole family would suffer.

I looked at the car sitting in Ethan's driveway. Car.

Singular. As in only one. Fuck. I spun around, light snow wafting down from the cold, gray sky, at the sound of my name being called from behind.

"You want me to take you home?" Ethan shouted from his front door.

I shrugged because right then I had no idea what I wanted or where to go or what to do.

"It's just all too much, you know?" I shouted at him. "I'm not ready for life. I'm supposed to be by now, but I'm not." I threw my hands into the air, ready to lie down in his yard and just give up. "I'm just… it's too much. I don't want to do this anymore, Ethan."

"Do what?" he yelled back, the snow starting to pick up in intensity.

"Adulting."

He snorted so loudly I heard it down by the car. "Welcome to life, my love. Can you come back inside? We can play Clue or something, maybe build some Lego Star Wars stuff, or watch cartoons. I could use a day of childhood again too. My leg aches, my neck is stiff, and I can't read the fine print in this stupid book I'm pretending to read."

I shuffled back to the open door, walked into his arms, and leaned all my weight into his chest as he hugged me tightly.

"Sorry for walking out," I said into the warm flesh of his neck. He ran a hand up and over my head, to keep my nose tight to his throat.

"It's okay. I'm sorry for piling things onto you. Can we talk about things? The notes, the hockey, the school, the boyfriend?"

"The boyfriend doesn't need talking about. He just needs to cue up some *Fairly Oddparents* and let me veg for a few hours." I burrowed into him, slipping my arms around his waist, feeling the solid strength of him taking on my weight and my worries. "The boyfriend is the best part of all that adult stuff."

"Glad to hear it." He pressed a kiss to my ear, eased out of my arms, and closed the door on the nosy neighbors.

Within minutes, we were on the sofa, candy and soda in hand, watching cartoons that I'd watched back when life was nothing more than animated nonsense, junk food, and the joy of hockey being played for hockey's sake. True to his word, he didn't broach the subject of the notes all day. When it was finally discussed, it was me who brought it up after we'd been in bed for a bit, his back pressed to my chest, my hand rubbing the hairs that trailed down under his navel to his junk. He'd been tender and open tonight, rolling to his back and pulling me on top. He'd wanted me inside him, he'd said. He was giving and mouthy, his comments sinful and snarly as I rocked into him, then slid out, over and over, until he urged me to stop treating him like an old man with a bum leg and fuck him.

"But you *are* an old man with a bum leg," I panted, wiggling to the side a bit and placing that bum leg gently to the side so I could hoist his good leg up over my shoulder.

That made him chuckle, but just for a second. Then his laughter turned into low, gruff groans of pleasure. I did that to him, for him, made him groan and growl and undulate until we were both lost in our orgasms.

"I don't know what to do about them," I whispered a

long while later, my fingertips moving over his treasure trail, his hand resting on my forearm.

"We talking about those notes?" He sounded drowsy. Great sex followed by a hot shower will do that.

"Yeah, I mean…" I closed my eyes and kissed his shoulder. "They scare me, Ethan." There. The confession was out there, floating around in the darkness of his bedroom. "Life scares me. I used to be so confident, knowing that I could do it all, handle whatever the world threw at me. My freshman year here? Man, it was all about confidence. Now? Now I move through life scared of what will fall out of the sky onto me next. Failing school terrifies me. Not making the team terrifies me. Losing you terrifies the living shit out of me. Those fans in Michigan terrified me. And now this asshole sending me letters…"

"I know, life is fucking scary. It's not just you. We're all moving through our days scared that something will change, someone will die, something dear will be lost. I lie here at night, when you're not here, and I can't catch my breath for the fear of what lies ahead. Hockey is all I know. What am I going to do now that I can't play hockey? What about us? What am I going to do with the next fifty years of my life? Will you head off for some remote Canadian town?"

"Not sure you'd call Edmonton remote," I had to gently point out.

"Place has moose; it's remote."

"There are moose in Minnesota."

"Stop talking facts to me. I'm trying to explain about my worries, and you're giving me moose-housing facts."

That made me chuckle loudly. I loved that about him.

How he could bring in some humor to the direst of discussions and make them feel less heavy. He lifted my hand from his lower belly and kissed the back of my fingers. I loved it when he did that too. "What I'm trying to say is that we all face down those demons every day. Sometimes you can let things go. God knows I procrastinate all the time, but those notes, babe, those are downright creepy. You cannot let that person continue terrorizing and threatening you. You say you're scared of life? Well, maybe if you start being proactive and stop letting others hurt you that fear might lift a bit."

"Yeah, maybe…"

"Sleep on it." He kissed the pad of my thumb. "I'll be right by your side through it all."

"Promise?"

"Totes my goats."

I snickered right beside his ear. "No one says that anymore."

"You sure? I saw a meme the other day on Facebook. It was this tote with a goat in it, and it reminded me of how much I like saying that." He nibbled on my index finger, his tongue soft and warm as it moved over the tip. "Think I and Jared should form a group for old puck pushers who are sleeping with younger puck pushers. We could sit around, talk about the glory days, and toss out old sayings that make our men groan with shame."

"So it would be exactly what you and Jared do now when you meet up?"

"God, you are such a wiseass." He tongued a wet line over my palm. "Don't let things with those notes go on too long, okay? I'm not trying to pressure you. I'm just concerned. You need to be safe to ensure that you can help your family out."

What a shitter. He'd used some major psychology on me there. "Yeah, I know. You're right." He muttered something that sounded like he agreed that he was right. I let my head rest on the pillow, keeping him tight to me, as I waited for sleep to slip up and carry me off. I didn't lie there long. I was mentally rundown.

It felt like only five minutes had passed when the sound of shattering glass woke both Ethan and me up. Brutally cold air blew into the bedroom as we floundered around slapping at the lights on the nightstands. There on the carpet, among the busted glass, lay a stone Santa gnome that we'd bought in town a week ago. Tied to the gnome who had been on the front porch was a pink envelope. My skin crawled, and my stomach heaved. No, no, not again…

"What the fuck?" Ethan gasped, leaving the warm bed, nude, to wobble around.

"Watch where you walk. There's glass all over," I said, sliding from the covers and into a pair of lounge pants. "Just sit down before you fall over."

"What the *fuck*!" he roared, dropping to the edge of the mattress while I searched for some slippers, his jogging pants, and his cane. "What the ever-loving fuck!" I had no words, so I said nothing. What could I say? This was on me. Totally. The person had been here. Skulking around Ethan's house. I tossed some sweatpants, socks, and his blue cane at him, then made for the gnome.

I yanked the note free from the ribbon, ripped it open, and unfolded it with trembling hands.

· · ·

U R MINE. *HE IS DEAD NOW. U SEE.*

"CALL THE POLICE," I croaked around the fear lodged in my throat.

TWELVE

Ethan

OFFICER LOU MITCHAM WAS THOROUGH. I'LL GIVE HIM that. His brother-in-law was a builder and called him to come over to board up the window as soon as he saw the mess. Of course he asked me if that was okay, but I had a hundred things in my head, and there was no room to think about securing the house. I had Benoit, who hadn't moved from the sofa, and he was my priority. I sat next to him as Officer Mitcham took photos of the scene, while his partner made plans for the morning to canvas my closest neighbors for copies of their security footage. Benoit had the notes he'd retrieved from his drawer upstairs, on his lap, and he clutched them so tight they bent at the edges. I eased his grip open, and after a moment's wrestling, he let go of them, and I put them on the small coffee table next to the letter from the gnome sealed in an evidence bag.

"Okay then, let's start this from the beginning." Officer Mitcham sat on the sofa opposite and looked at us expectantly. "Do you know who might be responsible for this?"

"No," Benoit said, and he sounded so miserable that I took his hand again. If Officer Mitcham had an issue with two men holding hands, he didn't show it.

"What about you, Mr. Girard?"

I started at the use of my name. "Me?"

"High-profile hockey player announces retirement, a super fan who sees you with Mr. Morin and thinks that you should have looked at them instead?"

"The note was meant for me," Benoit murmured and pushed the folder toward Officer Mitcham. "There's more of them, all the same tone, decreasing in logic each time."

Officer Mitcham opened the folder, and for the first time, I saw the Post-it on each one with a date and place, and also a time when Benoit had found them.

"You've received all of these notes?"

Benoit nodded. "At first there was coherence about them; they talked about summer and loving me, and then they gradually grew worse, and now a gnome through our window."

"Do you live here, Mr. Morin?"

"No," Benoit said and sounded horrified, as if it was a bad thing that he might even think of living with me. That was shit, but then I'd fallen for someone who was fiercely independent.

"So we could hypothesize that this is someone who knows you and Mr. Girard are friends, and maybe followed you here tonight? Would that be an accurate assessment?"

Next to me, Benoit groaned and shook off my hand so he could press fingers to his temples.

By the time the officers had left, the window had been boarded up, and Benoit had made a full statement. He'd spoken about the notes, the jeering at the hockey game, assured the sympathetic officer that he was sure the two weren't related, and then as soon as we were on our own, he slumped onto the sofa and tilted his head back, his eyes closed. They'd taken the letters as evidence, they had a statement that covered everything, and now it was just him and me.

"I'm not leaving," I said and sat next to him. Officer Mitcham had suggested we go to a hotel, but I wasn't backing down. "But if you feel you want to go home, I wouldn't blame you."

"I'm okay here, if that's okay with you?" He was unsure, and I needed to stop that now. I stumbled to my feet and pulled him with me.

"I want you to stay, and I have one more call to make before I'm going back to bed." He sat with me as I called Brady.

"It's four a.m., asshole," Brady grumped.

I didn't even stop to apologize and hoped to hell Brady would understand; after all what were best friends for? "I've got some trouble here. When you had that thing with your brother, the security you hired, who was it?"

I could imagine Brady going from half-asleep and pissed at me to sitting upright in bed. "What happened?" he demanded, and I heard rustling and movement as it appeared he left the bedroom. I'd never even checked if Boston were playing away or if he was at home.

"I'm sorry, Brady. Are you at home?" I began, but he made a noise of irritation.

"Yes, but you call me at dawn. It's gonna be important. Now, start again."

Okay, I could do this. I didn't have to lose my shit right

now. "When Ten was in the hospital, there was a security company you hired that watched over him, and I need their number so they can—I mean, I don't need protection, but maybe Benoit… or I can get them out here to fix cameras." Christ, I was making absolutely no sense at all.

"Calm down, E, and tell me what happened."

"Later. Right now, do you have a number, Brady?"

I just needed a contact, and then I could sit with Benoit and work my damn hardest to alleviate the fear in his eyes.

"No," Brady said, "it wasn't an official thing. It was something that Stan Lyamin arranged."

I thought on my feet. Stan Lyamin? I didn't have the Railers' goalie's number, but I did have Ten's, but maybe given the time right now, what I should be doing is not hassling anyone at all. Owatonna must have security companies. I should just leave this until the morning. Then I checked Benoit, saw the defeat in his expression, and hardened my resolve.

"Can you get Ten to—?"

"I'm texting you Stan's number," Brady interrupted, and my phone vibrated with the number arriving. "Just tell me everything is okay right now and that I shouldn't call other friends in Minnesota to go over to your place with their sticks."

I wanted to laugh. I think Brady was attempting to lighten the tone, but Benoit looked sick, and when I caught his gaze, he offered me a shaky smile. "It will be."

By five a.m., I had spoken to Stan, had not understood much of what he was saying, apart from that I should expect a visit from a guy called Gavrie who would be there at ten a.m., and in Stan's words. "He fix."

I'm sure Stan didn't mean only the windows. After all,

I'd explained I was fearful of my partner's well-being, and he'd listened to all of it before releasing a stream of Russian.

Benoit and I didn't sleep much more, and I ended up driving him back to his house just before six. He had a test today.

"You need to tell the professor that you've had no sleep—"

He stopped me from talking, with a kiss.

"I'm good," he said, and I admired him for what was either bravery or sheer pigheadedness. Probably a combination of both. I watched him walk up to his front door, hyper-alert to anyone hanging around, and wondering what the hell I was checking for. The security footage from my own shitty camera showed nothing more than a hooded figure in blurred gray and white. No way was anyone getting an ID from that grainy shit. Why weren't security cameras like the ones on TV that gave full facial details at the push of a button? We couldn't even tell if it was a girl or a boy or how big they were.

I ended up going home a little after ten. A tall man, with tattoos on his hands, waited on the porch, not wearing a coat, and with an expression that was probably scaring off the icy cold Minnesota winter. "Gavrie," he announced firmly in an accent that sounded very Russian. "GBK Security. You have fifteen easy ways to get into this house."

"It's a rental," I defended as if that made it any better.

He muttered something under his breath. "No excuse," he said louder. Then he strode up to the door and with a twist of metal rod, he was in my hallway, holding the door open and waiting for me. "You want to see other ways?"

I felt faintly sick. NHL players don't always get the attention that football and baseball stars get. I'd had my share of groupies who'd followed me around, but that had been in my younger days. I'd never thought I'd have any kind of stalker who would want to go to the effort of getting into my house. I wasn't stupid though. I mean, I'd done my due diligence on the security in this house. The door locked with a key, there was a deadbolt, the windows locked, and I had an alarm and a security camera. I was safe. Of course the alarm hadn't even been turned on last night. *Stupid.*

I'd never felt this vulnerable before, and I knew it was because the thought of someone I loved getting hurt was a knife to the gut. Were we too obvious? Had Benoit been right? Maybe we should have never even started any of this? Maybe I should have stayed away and not fallen in love so fast, and maybe—

"We got this." Gavrie clapped a meaty hand on my shoulder. "No more sad face."

There was a knock at the door, and Gavrie pushed past me to answer it with a bellowed "Can I help?"

I recognized one of my neighbors, an elderly former lawyer who kept his lawn perfect and mine as well where it butted up against his. Jim Reynolds had an opinion of the kind of renters there had been in the house before, and all of a sudden, he was confronted with one commanding Russian and the cops arriving in the night. Things didn't look good.

"Jim," I blurted as I managed to lever my way past Gavrie. "Everything okay?"

He smiled at me, holding out his palm. "The officer last night said I should keep an eye on things out here, and

I was clearing snow by your path, and I found this. I don't know if it's yours?"

I stared down at the key dangling from a yellow ribbon on his palm and shook my head. "I don't recognize it."

Jim shook his hand. "It was on your property. I think maybe the officers might like to see it?"

I took it from him and placed it carefully on the hall table, noticing that Gavrie was hanging out just inside the kitchen door, peering around the corner. I pulled the front door closed a little and blocked the entrance.

"Sorry about last night, Jim."

"Not at all," Jim announced and rubbed his hands together. "It's the most excitement we've seen down here since the barbecue of oh-seven. Is everything okay? I saw you drive your boyfriend away, and he wasn't smiling like he usually does."

I didn't know what to do with that observation. When did neighborly concern cross over to something vaguely unsettling? Not that I thought Jim was the stalker, but fuck, I felt like I was living in a fishbowl.

"He's fine," I lied.

"Well, I wanted to say to you that the police took our security footage or downloaded it at least. We have a system that backs up to the cloud."

My cell vibrated, and I mentally thanked the god of phone calls, if there was even such a thing. I pulled it out with an apologetic smile, seeing Brady's name there.

"I'm sorry, work. I have to take this. Thank you for the key you found."

"No problem." Jim didn't seem put out at all. "You know where I am if you need me."

I was suddenly so grateful for having a neighbor who

actually showed an interest in me and my house. When Benoit and I finally bought a place together, wherever he ended up, then it would have to be in a community where people talked to each other.

"Thank you, Jim." And I meant it. I connected the call to Brady as I shut the door, and then I had to go through the entire night in painfully minute detail; never let it be said that Brady wasn't as thorough as the cop had been when he'd taken our statements.

When I headed for the rink, I was done with the house, with explanations, and with the way that Gavrie kept poking around the house and sending me death glares of disappointment.

"Rented," I reminded him when he commented pointedly on the ease with which he could lift the patio door from its seating. I could have pointed out that normal human beings couldn't lift the weight, but it wasn't worth it.

At least at the rink, it was quiet, the ice smooth, the noise of skates, a couple of the team using downtime from studies to get some work in. I saw two of them were a D-pair, and laced up my own skates. Nothing like working with budding defensemen to get my head straight.

HEADING UP TO BENOIT'S PARENTS' place for Christmas was exactly what we needed. The fact that the police had no ideas about who was sending the letters had both of us on edge, and despite the extra security at my place, we ended up spending a lot of our downtime at the shared house. That was the best of things and the worst of them as well. Privacy was at a premium, but then seeing Benoit with his friends was a good thing. He was lighter with them around, whereas I think I reminded him of the whole mess with the letters. He hadn't received any more, or at least that I knew about, and I hoped he would be honest if he did. I knew why he hadn't told tell me before, but now everything was in the open, I wanted to know everything that happened to him.

The flight to Quebec City was long, but it gave us plenty of time to just be us. To chill and watch crappy movies. The more distance we put between us and Owatonna, the better. He relaxed little by little and grew more excited with each mile closer to his home. No one was meeting us at the airport. His mom had wanted to, but she'd switched shifts at the last minute, so it had been up to us to rent a car, and we headed north out of the city.

The snow towered above each side of the cleared roads, and we made good time, listening to local radio stations and adding our own voice-overs when the radio was nothing more than crackling silence.

Notre-Dame-du-Portage was a small town on the banks of the St Lawrence River, a stunning place, all white houses and small churches set into rocks down to the water. The road we took headed around the back of the town, where the houses were closer, and the sidewalks not quite as cleared.

"Take a left," Benoit said, and I followed the instructions, taking a wide angle around a snowbank. "Stop up here." He pointed to a parking lot, but it wasn't by a house but by a small lake. He unbuckled and climbed out of the car, grabbing his coat and gesturing for me to follow. Dressed against the cold, hats on, gloves, layered scarves, we ended up standing by a small fence that surrounded the space.

"White Fish Lake," he said and grinned widely. "This is where I learned to skate." He slipped his gloved hand into mine. "Dad would bring me out here, and I was maybe four? Five? I don't know, but I had these tiny skates, and I'd spend all day out here, bundled up, racing up and down so fast. At least I thought I was fast, but when you look back at the family videos, it was more of a stumble drag-step." He laughed, and I had to kiss him next to his lake. I just had to. He tasted of the chocolate we'd eaten in the car, and I loved the taste of him so much it hurt.

"When did you start skating without drag-steps?" I asked and pulled him into my side.

"I don't know. It just happened. Then, one day, there were a load of us out there, and no one wanted to be in goal, and so we took it in turns with this borrowed gear, and when the other kids just screamed and laughed, I wanted to do it and take it seriously."

"I bet you stopped everything getting in that net."

He huffed a laugh. "Nah, I was a sieve, worse than a sieve, but you know, after that first day, I would push and push. I watched goalies, a lot of my personal hero Malcolm Subban."

"He's a good kid." I realized what I'd said when Benoit side-eyed me.

"He's older than me," he teased, and I hip-checked him enough so he nearly fell in the snow. "But his brother, PK, he came out with a video, talking to a skater who'd been getting grief from fans for the color of his skin." Benoit paused and half closed his eyes. "I want to get this right because it's important. PK said in January that we've got to believe in ourselves and let nobody tell us what we can and can't do, especially if it's because of the color of our skin. It means something that I have role models, and I want to get selected by Edmonton and be that to someone else."

Watching Benoit talk with such passion, I wanted to kiss him again, but he was still talking.

"That whole *Spiderman* thing, you know, with great power comes great responsibility? I want to make a difference to kids who don't fit inside the lines, where the color of their skin may make them stand out, or they may not come from families with money, or they might be gay or bi. And I forget that in Owatonna when I let everything else drag at me. I need to think about the big picture." He shook his head and smiled so hard. "I sound like a giant dork."

I couldn't help but tease him then. "Word of advice. If you're going to climb buildings, you may want to take your pads off." Then I kissed him again, *just because*, before tugging him back to the car. "Come on, Spidey, it's meet-the-parents time."

THIRTEEN

Benoit

SOMETIMES WHEN A PERSON SITS BACK AND LOOKS
around, they realize how lucky they've had it. Watching
my family welcome Ethan into our home and our lives
openly choked me up. Yes, I'd faced some crap and was
still dealing with a huge problem, but overall, on the life
scale, I'd had it good. My family accepted me and my new
boyfriend. That right there was huge. I knew quite a few
queer kids whose family wanted nothing to do with them.
Trans kids who had no home to return to over the holiday
breaks. I was damn lucky.

"Okay, really, enough hanging on the man," I finally
said laughingly as I waded in to save Ethan from my
mother, father, and sister. They'd had him pinned in the
kitchen for an hour, stuffing him with sponge cake and
coffee. "We're going to go unpack. I'll get Ethan settled.
Then I'll head down to the basement and pull out the
sofa." I yawned to drive home the point.

"Why on earth would you want to sleep in the
basement?" Dad asked, carefully getting to his feet with

the help of two canes. "It's colder than a witch's boob down there."

"You could have said tit, Dad. I've heard that word before," Tamara tossed out as she reached for another slice of homemade sponge cake.

"Not from me you haven't," Dad replied, giving me a wink. "You two sleep in your room. Mom and I are fine with it as long as you don't wake us up when you get jiggy with it."

"Oh. My. God." I felt the heat rush to my face. "We don't 'get jiggy with it.'" I looked at my mother. She was hiding a snicker behind her coffee mug.

"We don't?" Ethan asked. I wanted to slap him. Instead, I grabbed his wrist and pulled him to his feet. "Guess we're taking a nap now. He's really pushy. Did you raise him to be so pigheaded, or was he born that way?"

"Born that way," all three of my family members replied simultaneously. Then they laughed.

"Ha-ha." I tugged Ethan along, up the stairs to my old room, after grabbing our bags from the foyer. "Why would you tell them we're having sex?"

"You think they don't know?"

Ugh. Yes, of course they did. I just… it made me itchy to imagine my mother thinking of me being fucked in the ass by Ethan. I heard his chuckle behind me and ignored it.

"This is my room. Don't be intimidated." I threw open the door, stepped inside, and waited for him to limp inside.

"Wow, it's a shrine. A goalie shrine. I feel like I should light a candle and drop to my knees, which I would do, but well, one bad leg and all that."

I smiled at him, my gaze roaming over the posters and

sticks on the blue walls. My heroes. The men who had made me want to emulate them on the ice and off.

I tossed our bags to the corner, opened the drapes, and sat on the double bed. "I used to lie here in bed at night as a kid and stare at Grant Fuhr and know that I had to be him someday. Like, not as good because he's a legend. First black player to win the Stanley Cup. First black player to be inducted into the Hockey Hall of Fame. So yeah, never that good. But maybe just a tenth as good. Then Malcolm came up and started playing." I waved at all the goalies on the wall. "I wanted to be him too. Still do."

Ethan smiled and cupped my face. "I love hearing you talk about the men you admire, the game you love, the plans that you have for yourself. I desperately want to be a part of your future."

I leaned in and put my mouth on his. The kiss was long, sweet, and wet. A promise of a future that I also desperately wanted, with him beside me.

"You could at least close the door," Tamara chided as she walked past on her way to her room. Again, my cheeks grew hot. And again, Ethan snickered at my embarrassment.

"She's such a brat," I mumbled, got up, and closed the door. "Let's unpack now. Then we can crash."

"How about you unpack and I nap. That sounds good. I'm old and infirm." He fell back over the bed, arms out, and made sickly old man sounds.

"Man, you will do *anything* not to have to pack or unpack, won't you?" He laughed lightly, so I started taking out the clothes of his that I had packed, neatly, yesterday. His idea of packing was to stand on one side of the room, wad up his clothes, and see if he could make a three-pointer. Dude was seriously not the least bit worried about his appearance.

"Packing is for camels," he replied. I arched an eyebrow but let it slide. I yanked open a deep bottom drawer on my dresser and felt nostalgia wash over me.

"I haven't seen this in ages," I murmured, lifting the old metal lockbox out of the drawer. "Hey, Geezer Joe, look at this."

I sat down beside him. He pushed up to a sitting position, then lifted the firebox from my hand. "I can see you've had a hand in decorating this." He tapped at the Edmonton logo drawn on the lid of the green steel box. "But I never pictured you as a unicorn sort."

"Oh yeah, well, I didn't draw that one. Dominque did."

"And Dominque is?"

"Dominque Wells. Dom we called her. Old girlfriend. My first girlfriend. We were sixteen and so in love, or so I thought. She never did quite grasp how I could love a violent game like hockey. She hated it when I billeted with a family in the States. Accused me of cheating on her when I didn't. I don't cheat. I have morals."

"Yeah, I know, babe." I gave him a flimsy smile.

"Guess you do. Anyway, before she got possessive, we made this time capsule thing, and we made a pact that we'd come back in ten years, still a couple, and open it. It's locked, though."

Ethan patted my thigh. "Cute story. The innocence of a first love. Was she cute?"

"Oh yeah, adorable. Dark red hair, freckles, bright blue eyes, great legs." I rattled the lockbox. "We put some true junk in here. A picture of us on the lake skating. She dreamed of being Tessa Virtue to my Scott Moir. She loved ice dancing and wanted me to give up hockey to skate pairs with her. And she was good, not Olympic skills of course, but good. We met at the lake. She skated right over to me during a shinny game and asked me out. We dated for a year before I broke it off."

"First loves rarely last," he said, giving my leg a squeeze.

"I know." I sighed, wondering what had ever become of that pretty little girl with the beautiful red hair. "Anyway, we put money inside, which was to be used for an apartment."

"How much money?"

I shook the box again, the coins inside rattling loudly. "A handful of loonies each. Man, we were so not prepared for the adult world."

Ethan yawned, and I followed suit. I tossed the box back into the dresser, then finished emptying our suitcases, stripped down to my underwear, and crawled into bed with him. He curled up behind me, chest to my back, and his soft snores eased me to sleep. My dreams were pleasant. Good times with old friends, Christmases past, Ethan and I in the future with a big yellow dog. The town we and our dog lived in was a lot like Edmonton. I prayed that dreams did come true.

THE CHRISTMAS BREAK went by far too fast. Ethan and I spent two weeks in Notre-Dame-du-Portage, and in all truth, I had to push myself to return to Owatonna. Mom's cooking, the sound of my father's laughter, the teasing lilt of my sister's jokes, and the happiness in Ethan's beautiful eyes made me yearn to stay here forever. We'd spent days eating, playing stupid board games, enjoying pick-up games with some of my old hockey chums, and lazing around in bed touching and kissing and making plans for that future with a yellow dog.

Sadly, the glow of Christmas was replaced by the second semester of my senior year. And the first week back on campus, I knew why Jacob and Hayne had been so fried last year. Ryker, Scott, and I were starting to look the same. January brought with it a heap of schoolwork and hockey. Studying and hockey—that was all I had time for. I needed to pick a senior thesis topic, work on my high glove side, and try to balance a relationship. Thank God, Ethan was so laid-back. He got me, got *it*, got the weight that was piling up class by class and game by game.

"So, what are you doing for your thesis?" Ryker asked one morning over breakfast. Ethan had made coffee and burned some toast for us. Hayne stepped in after waking up and saved us all with a pan of scrambled eggs, and ketchup. "My brain is unable to compute. I seriously need a tutor or something. How did it get to be the final semester? My head hurts."

"Is yours a one-or two-credit thesis?" I asked.

Ryker moaned and shrugged. "I don't know," he whimpered.

Scott patted his head and forked more eggs into his face.

"I can help anyone who needs it," Hayne said, sitting on his chair, legs to his chest, sipping some coffee and nibbling on burnt toast. "I did really well on mine last year. And I'm not inspired to paint, so I need something to do."

"Hey, I'll gladly take any help offered," Ryker moaned as he shook more ketchup onto his eggs.

Ethan made a face at the mess on my friend's plate but remained silent. He always seemed as if he felt out of odds with college talk, and I understood that. Hard to really grasp it when you'd never lived it.

"I think I have my topic narrowed down to Multiculturism in Education and How to Integrate it into the Classroom of the Future. What do you think? That sound like a good topic?"

Everyone nodded, even Ethan, so I felt a small weight of worry lift off my back. No sooner had I gotten that settled than my phone alarm went off, reminding me that I had an interview at The Aviary with a reporter from QYT —*Queer Youth Times*—a hip and trendy magazine that everyone who was LGBTQ or straight on campus read. They'd reached out to me several times after that mess in Michigan, and I'd put them off. Ethan, over our Christmas holiday, had persuaded me to do one interview. One sit-down that would cover the ugliness I'd faced and how, hopefully, one young kid would read it and see that we all faced hardship, but we battled past it.

I'd asked Ryker, who contacted the Railers' social media guy for assistance. Layton Foxx was sharp, knew everyone and everything, and had set the interview up with my chosen outlet in five minutes. Layton had agreed to handle the social media related to the story when it came out next month. I had no time to worry over Instagram and Facebook posts. I had school and hockey. The Frozen Four loomed ahead of us, and the Eagles were looking like real contenders.

"I have to get ready for this interview," I said, sighed, and got to my feet. "Dibs on the shower."

Ryker and Scott waved me off. Ethan had already hit the shower, so as soon as I was dressed and ready, we walked to the eatery, hand in hand, the winds of a Minnesota January sanding any exposed flesh with bits of ice and snow.

The place was empty, all the patrons either in classes or heading there. A young guy jogged over to me, rich brown skin and beautiful chocolate eyes, his black hair was styled into a deep undercut, and his teeth were white and straight. A beautiful man really, not much older than me. Bright rainbow scarf dangling from the lapels of a thick wool duster.

"It's so nice to meet you, Benoit. I'm Arjun Gokhale from *Queer Youth Times*. And you're Ethan Girard. A true pleasure. I grew up in Boston and got to see you and Brady Rowe play all the time. My dad is a season ticket holder."

"Pleasure. Why don't we sit down and get some coffee?" Ethan gestured to the empty tables. Within minutes, we were seated at a round table, coffee in hand, and a cell phone lying on the table recording everything that we said. Seeing that phone made me edgy.

"Listen, I know this interview is about empowerment, but can we not make me and Ethan a huge thing?" I asked, laying a hand over the phone to blot out my request. "We're not making a big announcement here, okay? We just are. You can say that we're dating, but don't make that the headline. I'm not here to titillate people with juicy gossip."

"Sure, that's cool. I'll merely make mention of Ethan sitting supportively but silently at your side," Arjun assured me, and I found the truth in his dark eyes. I removed my hand from the phone, nodded at him, and then took a deep breath.

Arjun was good at his job. He eased me into things with perfunctory questions about my past, how I came to play hockey, fun tidbits about my family, my best times as a hockey player, and then he slid right into the meaty part.

"So, we've touched on the best times you've had on ice. Care to fill us in on the not so good times? What exactly happened in Michigan? It's been a source of online discussion, and we'd like to know how you feel about being an African-American playing a game that's predominately filled with white men and fans."

"Okay first, I'm not African-American; I'm Canadian. I can only speak about my own experiences, not those of Black Americans, although we all suffer the same injustices."

"Oh, sorry, okay. I knew you were from Canada." He made a face at his gaffe. "I don't think we need to rehash the slurs. Our readers are familiar with them all. Do you feel as if you're getting hatred from both barrels being a queer man of color?"

I glanced at Ethan. He raised an eyebrow, sipped his coffee, and said nothing. Lots of help from that quarter. My gaze fell to the liquid in my mug as I mulled over my reply.

"I feel as if people need to stop worrying about who I take to bed or how much melanin my skin has." I glanced from my coffee to the reporter. "All I want to do is play hockey. I have to think that someday the color of a player's skin or their sexual identity won't matter. What *will* matter is playing the game you love for the joy of the game itself."

"Excellent. Do you have any advice for kids out there who are struggling with being ripped on for their race or sexual orientation?"

I nodded. "Just keep doing what you're doing. Live your life, eyes on the prize. If you want to be a teacher, an astronaut, a ballerina, or a hockey player, you keep that pride in yourself, and you do *not* let others squash your self-esteem. Believe in yourself and the goals you're working towards. And hey, I am online, although I'm the worst at social media, but if anyone out there is having trouble because of bigotry, just drop me a line, okay, and we can talk."

"And one final question. Who do you predict to win the Stanley Cup this year?" Arjun inquired. Ethan snorted into his cup at the expression on my face.

"Edmonton, naturally."

We chatted a bit more, and Arjun left after a handshake and a sincere thanks for allowing QYT to be the source I chose to speak with. He assured me that I'd know as soon as the magazine hit the racks. After he pushed back into the winter weather to return to Minneapolis-St. Paul where the home office was, I sat down and looked questioningly at Ethan.

"What do you think? Did I blow it? Or was I okay? Man, I hate interviews," I moaned, wishing I'd had better replies. Wittier ones. Ones that made me sound smart instead of like a dimwit.

Ethan sat up and kissed me on the lips. "You make me incredibly proud to be known as your boyfriend."

"Yeah?"

"Yeah."

Luck seemed to be on my side finally. So, feeling lucky and full of myself, I grabbed Ethan's coat lapels and yanked his mouth back to mine. To hell with the workers watching us from behind the counter. Life was good. Hell, life was more than good; it was great. And I wanted to share this wonderful new phase of my life with Ethan.

"Guys should be in class by now," I whispered over his kiss-slicked lips. "Want to go to my place and fool around until I have class?"

"When's your next class?"

I glanced at my phone on the table. "An hour and forty minutes."

"Check please!"

FOURTEEN

Ethan

I COULD TELL BENOIT WAS NERVOUS ABOUT THE INTERVIEW going live today, so I took him out on the ice to focus him, and because I really wanted to get back on the cold stuff.

"My damn leg is taking so long to heal." I said as I wobbled for the second time. I didn't do falling over. I was solid on my skates, but my leg felt weird. I think it would have been better if I had been on the team still. PTs would have been working with me so I could get back on the ice, but I thought I'd become a bit lazy these last few weeks. Even though I'd managed those few pickup games I wasn't steady yet.

"It's old age." Benoit smirked and skated backward, daring me to follow him. Which I did. He let me catch him, but given we ended up kissing in the empty rink, I think he might have done it deliberately.

The interview was posted, and, and by the evening, it had gained traction, picked up by several big ticket websites. In general, it was well received. Of course, there were comments from people who said that Benoit wasn't fit to play professional hockey, due to the color of his skin or his orientation. It wasn't a surprise—there would always be intolerant entrenched fans. For the most part, Benoit stayed away from the social media crap and instead listened with a soft smile as I read out the comments that were all about approval and acceptance. The other ones, the garbage ones, I kept those to myself.

We were up against a strong Falcons team this Saturday in Sioux Falls, the first West Regional game in our fight to win the NCAA Championship, aka the Frozen Four. One team wins college hockey's national title, every year, along with all the glory and kudos, but for that one team to win, fifty-nine others have to lose. In fact, only the sixteen best teams go through to this competition, and we'd made it through to the last sixteen by only one point. Four regional teams would meet, and the winner of that group would take one of the coveted final four places. We weren't the favorites by any stretch of the imagination, although everyone expected great things from Ryker and Benoit. Getting through to the next round was all the team could think about. Benoit included. He'd deliberately gotten ahead in his studies just so he could stop for the two days before the game, and he spent a hell of a lot of time either at the rink facing off against our dedicated forwards or working with me and the defensemen. Edmonton would be watching, as he was one of their picks, and he was desperate to get noticed and be given a place on the team.

I knew they'd want him this year. I felt it in my bones, and not only because I'd fallen in love with him and everything he did was pretty damn fine in my eyes. I'd seen his level of skill and focus before in top-line goalies

I'd gone up against in the NHL, and he had so much promise.

He had to focus, and I knew better than to disrupt what he had going on in his head. All I could do was try to make things easy for him; by cooking for him, which I loved, by keeping an eye on his schedule, which made me feel a little like his mom, and just by being there. It gave me something to focus on other than the fact that out there was someone who was watching him, *us*, and that I felt as if our lives were being invaded.

Thinking about being watched had made me cautious with the PDAs; not that we were hugely demonstrative in public. We weren't like Scott and Hayne, who regularly hugged and kissed anywhere they could. Still, even holding hands might mess with our stalker's head, so I'd backed off a little.

That hurt a lot, but it might just keep Benoit safe for a while until the cops tracked down whoever was sending the notes.

Benoit didn't have to worry about them at all, because I'd taken to checking for pink envelopes on an almost hourly basis, and we'd had all the locks changed in the guys' locker room, just so there was no chance something could be slipped in without us knowing.

I'd found two of them slipped through my front door. Two that Benoit didn't have to know about, that I gave straight to the cops. Ryker assured me there had been nothing at their place, so I guess the fact that Benoit was spending nearly every night with me was certainly being noticed by whomever was sending these damn letters. A week ago, the final security installation had been finished, four cameras on rotation and superior locking systems;

hell, it was as if we lived in Fort Knox, and I knew it made Benoit feel on edge, but I never made a big thing out of how he felt, and hid my own worries.

Today was our last practice before the first tournament game, and Coach Quinton was out there directing the team with all the calm self-assurance of a guy who instinctively knew his team was on fire. Everyone here had bought into his system, and the team crackled with barely contained excitement. I was envious of Coach; he was on the ice, getting into the center of the drills and creating chaos for the guys to work around. I'd seen this tactic before and wished more than anything I could be out there doing the same thing. I wanted Benoit prepared for the mess that would hit his crease; anything to keep him safe. Coach Quinton used his size and his stick to obstruct passes and made his players work around him to get the same job done. He was up in Benoit's face, and my man stood there and took everything thrown at him.

And now, here we were in Sioux Falls waiting for game one of this championship to start. Only two games stood between us and moving to the semi-finals. The Eagles wanted the win today, and they were restless and twitchy with unrestrained energy that made even the normally calm Ryker pace.

When they hit the ice for the game against the Hogs, they hit it hard and took the game to a three-goal lead after the first period.

"Okay, guys." Coach Quinton crossed his arms over his chest, and the entire team fell silent. I knew they were on a high because they were in the lead, but that was dangerous because it could lead to complacency. The Hogs hadn't come out fighting, but that would change.

"What do you think the Hogs' coach is in there saying to his team?" Coach Quinton asked.

"That they're losers," a voice called from the far end of the room. I didn't know who it was, but a couple of the guys snickered.

"Ryker?" Coach prompted.

The captain, with two of the three goals due to him, and the heart of this team, cleared his throat. "My guess is he'd be saying that Owatonna's ability to snarl up the Hogs' offense in the neutral zone and create turnovers on the forecheck is killing them." There were murmurs of agreement. "He'd be telling them that this isn't a practice and that they have to go out fighting in the second period."

"And Benoit?" Coach asked. "What is he telling them about our goalie?"

Benoit glanced up from where he'd been tapping a rhythm on his pads. "About me? Uhm... Well, it wouldn't be about me. More likely they're having their asses reamed and told they need more shots on goal. Right now, they're not even making it past our D to get to me. So yeah, they're probably being told to shoot whatever they can to get through."

Coach nodded. "Three goals in the first period? We're flying." He looked around the room, slowly, catching everyone's gaze. "But this is an elimination game, their only chance, and they will come out fighting now, fired up, ready to crash the crease, throw everything they can at Benoit, so keep focused, play the game, stick to the Owatonna way of playing. Everyone got that?"

There was a resounding "Yes, Coach," and the level of intensity in the room notched a little higher. I caught

Benoit's gaze as he passed me, and I winked at him. He smiled and led the team onto the ice for period two.

We were going to win this; I could feel it in my bones, and with the final score six-two with us taking the win, the locker room was ecstatic. No one wanted to say it, but the win had been a strong one, and I saw how dejected the Hogs had been as they'd left the ice.

The Eagles were in a hotel near the arena, and we took up almost an entire floor. I knew for a fact that Benoit was four doors down from me, sharing with Ryker, and I also knew there would be celebrations for the team but that I should stay away as I was one of the coaching staff. I wanted to go down and kiss him and hug him, but I didn't. We'd hugged in the locker room, and I'd congratulated everyone, not just Benoit. After all, the team was a step closer to the final, and that was all that mattered.

The knock didn't surprise me, though, but Benoit didn't come in when I opened the door. We weren't going to break rules, and we had our next game against a very strong side in the Cheetahs tomorrow. He needed sleep and focus.

I forced my hands into my pockets so I didn't reach out and yank him in. He copied the motion and gave me a wry smile.

"I miss you," he said, very simple and straight to the point.

"I miss you too," I replied.

He quirked a smile at me, and I gave him one of my trademark winks.

"Night," he murmured.

"Night," I said back and mouthed "I love you."

He briefly made a heart with his hands before he strode

down the hall to his room, letting himself in without looking back.

THE GAME against the Cheetahs was scrappy as hell and so close that for ninety percent of it I wasn't sure what the end score would be. Not only that, but now it was my turn to pace, and my leg muscles ached like a bitch. The break might have healed, but the affected muscles made me weak as a freaking kitten when it came to my trademark stride.

The score was three-two, in their favor, and Benoit had stopped so many shots that he had to have been dizzy with the amount of time nearly standing on his damn head. Coach wasn't happy, our defense was breaking, our forwards were falling into traps, we were completely off-plan, and it showed. I leaned on the wall next to the benches, listening to Coach calmly explaining how his team should *pull themselves together.* At least, that was what he was saying out loud, but I imagined the cursing he had going on in his head.

Two minutes left, we had shots on goal, and the tide shifted a little in our favor. Ryker's line went over the boards, and the Cheetahs were focused on him like flies on shit. In a scuffle the corner, it was the Cheetahs who had the puck, heading en masse toward Benoit, their captain confident, focused, collecting a rebound and wrapping around the back of the net. Benoit had him, stopped the shot easily, but it slithered from his grasp, bouncing off his blocker, and the Cheetah captain was right there, stick handling, trying to corral the bouncing puck, only he never quite got the hold of it, and Ryker was right in the scrimmage. It seemed to last forever, and then in a flash of brown and gold, Ryker had the puck and was skating like the wind down the rink. One D-man tried to hold him, another to trip him. He managed to avoid it all, and then with a maneuver that defied logic and gravity, he used his body to defend the puck, spun, deked, and shot. For a second the puck hung, or at least it felt that way to me, even though physics dictated it must be moving. Everything stilled, but their goalie had absolutely no way of switching direction fast enough to stop it, and when the goal horn sounded, the Owatonna fans rose in a wave of brown, creating a wall of shouts.

A tied game, and now only just over a minute left. This could go to overtime, and I wasn't sure my nerves could handle it. The tension was worse than any Stanley Cup final I'd been part of. I was invested in Benoit, and I felt everything, even though I wasn't on the ice and this wasn't *my* team. I felt hopeless as the clock ticked down. We needed another Ryker miracle, or for Benoit to make the save of his life to turn this game, or for any one of our other skaters to pull that one thing out of their hat which would give us the win. I wasn't ready for our journey to be over—I wanted this win for Benoit.

In the end, it didn't take a miracle. It didn't take our star player or our goalie. Fifteen-seconds to go, a check followed through by Shawn, the puck knuckling toward our goal, Cole Montgomery collecting through luck when one of the Cheetahs fell, and passing it hard to the opponents' net. Their goalie hadn't been expecting anything like it, and when the puck went past him, he looked as if he couldn't believe what had happened. As if the catalog of errors and misfortune hadn't just culminated in Owatonna going a goal up with only ten-seconds on the clock. I wanted to say that the Cheetahs rallied and fought for their lives in those remaining seconds, but they were in shock, and when the goal horn sounded, it was Owatonna who were through to the Frozen Four semi-finals by only one goal.

It was brown and gold that hugged and whooped in celebration, and scarlet that left the rink in complete despair.

We were through to the next round; we were going to Boston for the National Semi-finals.

THE MOOD on the four-hour drive back to Owatonna ranged from exuberant to exhausted to quiet. There were moments in those two games when the Eagles had shone; others where they had needed to work, and there had been back slaps, worries, pointers, and then tiredness. When we disembarked, I expected Benoit to head out with his housemates, thinking he would need to be around them. Instead, he walked with me, our hands brushing, until we made it back to the car. I didn't question where he wanted to be; I know I wanted him with me, but I also wanted to be the kind of partner who understood and who was supportive and not insanely greedy to be with him all the time.

He was quiet in the car, and the stillness unsettled me so much that I flicked on the radio, the soft sounds of a late night show drifting into the silence.

"That was some game," Benoit finally offered when we were only about ten minutes or so from the house. Did he want to talk? I could do that, but only if he wanted me to.

"It was a brilliant game," I said and indicated left off the turnpike.

"And lucky. I mean, we had some lucky bounces. That last goal..." He stopped talking and then reached over and placed his hand on mine. "Sometimes luck just happens, doesn't it?"

Was he talking about the game? Or us?

"It does." I thought that was the safest response until I knew the direction of this conversation.

"Like us," he mused and leaned his head back on the headrest. "I mean, it was lucky you broke your leg, which meant you came here and retired, and we met."

We pulled up to a stop light, and I couldn't help but tug him closer to kiss him in the dark. Everything was perfect right now, and when the lights changed and the car behind had to press his horn to get us to move, we were both laughing, even as I held up a hand in apology. Turning into the road leading to my house, I felt lighter than I had in a while. We'd won, Benoit was happy, and we were in love. I glanced to smile at him, and it was obvious he was just as happy.

The thud of something hitting the windshield, the crack of glass, and Benoit's horrified shout as I yanked the wheel to take us to the curb was chaos in my head, and I held up a hand to protect my eyes as glass shattered around me and momentum slammed me back into the headrest.

"Ethan!

FIFTEEN

Benoit

_____

IT ALL HAPPENED SO QUICKLY THAT MY ALREADY SLUGGISH mind had trouble linking things up. The car jumped the curb a second after something big had shattered the windshield. I threw my hands up to brace myself from hitting the dash. Instinct I guess, even though my seat belt was on. I yelled for Ethan as glass blew in through the massive hole, with bitter, cold air. I closed my eyes but not in time to avoid something small and sharp getting under my eyelid. The car slammed into something solid, snapping the seat belt across my chest and engaging the airbags. The back-and-forth motion made my head spin. Face full of bag, the inside of the car filled with acrid dust, and several car chimes went off at once.

"God, ah God." I coughed, my eye left eye weeping badly, my lungs filled with airbag dust, and my neck sore from the whiplash of back and forth. "Ethan, you okay?"

I swatted at the deflating airbag, the pain in my eye growing worse every time I blinked. "Ah, my eye, fuck!"

"My leg," he moaned as I shakily unbuckled my seat

belt, my watering eyes making it hard to see in the dark interior. "I think… oh yeah, it's fucked up again."

"Shit, shit. I'm calling for help." I wiped the back of my hand over my eye, dug my phone out, and kicked my door open, then crept around the car, yanking on Ethan's crumpled door. It was jammed up pretty badly, but finally the latch gave, and it creaked open.

"We sideswiped a tree," I said, working with him to get his seat belt unbuckled. "Your head okay?"

"Yeah, yeah, hard as granite. Ouch, fucking A that motherfucking, cock-sucking, furry-assed leg hurts like a humper."

The latch popped. I reached in and slid my hands under this arms, ready to back away and pull him free of the mangled wreck. "I can tell you're a hockey player."

He grunted as he wiggled around in the seat. I heard someone running up to me.

"My boyfriend needs help," I shouted to whoever was approaching.

"No, no, no boyfriends! You're mine!" A female screamed, leaping onto my back and battering me around the head with small, painful fists. I fell backward, dropping Ethan to the frosty ground, waving my hands to try to grab the wild woman on my back. She hit me in the face, hard, right in the same eye that was watering so badly. It hurt like hell. I wiped at my eye with my fingers, pulling them away, then staring at the blood on my fingertips as my feet went out from under me. "You fucked him! You said you loved me, but you left me, and then you fucked *him!* He has to die," she seethed, slapping at my face as I tried capture her hands. A sound blow to the side of my face made my ear ring.

We slid to the ground, and I rolled over and on top of my attacker. Headlights illuminated the yard. Vision blurred terribly, I blinked at the familiar face looking at me from inside a dark hoodie.

"Dom?" I croaked, the rush of new information coming into my stunned brain kind of stalling somewhere in the aftershock of a car crash. What? How was it my old ex was here?

People began shouting. Who they were I didn't know. Probably the folks who lived in the house whose tree we'd just run into.

Then someone pulled me off my ex, barking orders for me to lie on the ground facedown, hands behind my back. I knew a cop when I heard one, so I did as asked, no questions. I tried to explain why the black guy was manhandling the little white girl, but for some reason, I don't think he believed me. My mother did not raise a fool. I went lax and let him do his thing.

I allowed him to yank me to my feet, slap cuffs on me, and then haul me to the nearest police cruiser. Ethan bellowed at the cop who was leading me to the car. That was what threw a wrench into my impending arrest. That, and the fact that Dom was beating on a cop and screaming that I was her one true love and that the asshole who stole me had to die. Paramedics arrived, people milled around in robes and coats, and throughout it all, I could hear Ethan demanding that I be released right this fucking minute. God, I loved that man. It took some explaining, but I was finally released into the custody of the paramedics while Dom was led to a police cruiser, her long red hair having broken free from the tight bun under her hoodie. Her once smiling blue eyes now held nothing but hatred. She spit at me as two burly state troopers led her to their car.

I ran to Ethan after having a chunk of glass the size of a small pebble rinsed from my eye by an EMT. He applied some antibiotic drops, bandaged it, and threw up his hands as I broke free from his ministrations to go to Ethan. He was just being placed on a gurney. I checked his car and thought it was probably totaled. There on the console between us was a big chunk of cinderblock, and tied to the block, a damn pink envelope. I nearly threw up. We could have died. Both of us. She could have killed us both. My knees almost folded, but I held it together and went to Ethan, grabbing his hand as he reached for me.

"You okay? Are you okay?" I asked, the tears appearing, which made my eye burn. "I can't... she was... are you okay?"

"Yeah, good, fine. I think I rebroke my leg. Can you imagine?" His laugh was short, more of a bark of pain than a real laugh. "Just got the fucking cast off. What happened to you? Are you hurt?"

"Nope, no, just a bit of debris in my eye. It'll be fine." I squeezed his hand tightly. A cop car peeled off, the one with my old girlfriend in the back. Ethan began chirping the paramedic about his purple hair between groans of pain. I crawled into the back, ignoring the look from the paramedic who had tended to my eye. "I'm riding with him." It was not a polite request as one would expect from a good Canadian boy. It was a command. They all nodded as Ethan was loaded in.

We left the scene of the accident, police right behind us, and spent the next six hours in Our Lady of Perpetual Care hospital. Ethan had been X-rayed and casted and was now resting comfortably, an overnight stay a precaution as he had complained of a slight headache.

I was staring at the back of two police detectives as they left the waiting room. They seemed to have enough information from me about what had happened. Combined with the previous call about the stalking and Dom's rambling manic confession and fingerprint matches for all the notes, it seemed as though they had a good case against her. They'd asked me about a key that the neighbor had found outside Ethan's place. Since I knew nothing of this key, I told them that. One of them, an old white guy whose name I'd blanked on, showed me a picture of it on his phone.

Tired as I was, sore and in pain, it took me a second and a half to recognize that small gold key on a bright yellow ribbon. It was to the lockbox in my room. I'd kept the box, and Dom had kept the key. I still nursed the feeling of being gut-punched. Why hadn't Ethan told me about the key? Maybe I could have avoided all of this agony if I'd known about it and what it symbolized. The cops might even have been able to pick her up.

"Hey, you want more coffee?"

I blinked my one good eye at Ryker. I'd called him as soon as we'd arrived because I honestly didn't know if I'd need a ride home or a lawyer or perhaps both. His dad was well known and, I figured, able to summon an attorney in the middle of the night. Also, I just wanted to have a friend nearby during the questioning. Not that I'd done anything wrong, but I was shaky and felt sick. His presence had been reassuring.

"Thanks, sure." I gave him the empty cup in my hand, and he passed over a fresh cup. Then he sat beside me. "I can't get my head around all this. Like…" I stared down into my cup of joe. "I dated that woman."

"Yeah, it's wild. I've had exes that were mental, but not like legally mental, just socially mental. This Dom girl? Wow, she must have tracked you for years." He took a sip of his coffee, then fell silent.

"Guess so. Somehow she found me and… I don't know, started this hate campaign. I just… my head hurts." I got to my feet, Ryker glancing up at me with tired, worried eyes. "I need to walk."

"Okay, just be careful. You can't see right. Might walk into a wall or something." He motioned to the new gauze, padding, and eyepatch I now sported. "Or maybe the *Black Pearl* will sail up, and you'll have to fight Jack Sparrow for the honor of wearing the pirate captain crown."

"You're an asshole. I love you, but you're an asshole." I punched his knuckles with mine. Dude could joke, now that he knew Ethan was okay and I'd be back on the ice sometime. That *sometime* kind of worried me as I had tournament games to play and an NHL team to impress, but the ER doc said that the laceration was pretty deep but, on the flip side, eyes healed quickly. If I used the drops, applied the steroid cream, and took some Advil for the pain, I should be fine within two weeks. The team ophthalmologist had already been notified, and I was to be monitored closely for signs of infection.

I strolled down the hall and made a left, stopping to stare out at the new morning creeping over Minnesota. My body was ready for sleep, but my head kept spinning things around, trying to make sense of everything.

"Mr. Morin, we've gotten Mr. Girard settled into a private room, and he's asking for you." I waved her on. We rode up a few floors, her white shoes squeaking on the newly mopped floor tiles as she led me to room 314. "We'll be bringing up breakfast within the hour. Would you like a tray?"

I glanced around the corner at Ethan. He was as wiped out as I felt. And so alone. "Yeah, thanks. And can you give this to the young guy with the head of dark curls in the waiting room?" I dug into my pockets and found a crumpled twenty-dollar bill. "Tell him to eat something at the cafeteria and that as soon as breakfast is over, we can go home. His name is Ryker Madsen."

"Of course. Now try not to excite the patient. He's been drowsy but unable to fall asleep, and rest really would be beneficial to you both." She patted my biceps and squeaked off down the hall.

"You hitting on the nurses?" Ethan asked as I slid into the white-and-blue room. "Your eye?"

"Will be okay. Your leg?"

"Broke again, right along the same fracture line. Tree impact will do that to a bone. I talked to the cops. Benoit, I just don't know what to even say. That Dom girl, she seems unbalanced."

"Yeah, that's one way of putting it." I sat beside him on the bed, staring at the dried blood on my shirt and jacket. My blood. "I'm sorry you got caught up in it all. This is going to be a huge shitstorm. Ryker is keeping an eye on social media, says it's all on the down low now, but as soon as everyone wakes up. BOOM." I made a motion with my hands of a bomb going off. "All I wanted was to play hockey and love you on my own terms."

"I know, babe, I know. Sometimes life isn't dealt to us on our terms, though. If it was, I wouldn't be lying here with another cast on my stupid leg. I'd be home in bed loving you." I smiled at that. Loving him sounded good. So, so good. "Want to grab a few Z's with me before they bring breakfast?"

I toed off my shoes and cuddled up beside him, careful of the brilliant, white cast.

"You feel okay to talk a bit?" I asked, resting my hand on his chest. He gave me a slow nod. "There was a key found. Outside your place. Why didn't you tell me about it? I recognized it instantly. Dominique kept it on the same damn hair ribbon that I'd pulled from her hair and slid the key onto the day we'd made that time capsule in a box. I just... why didn't you tell me about it?"

His eyes drifted shut for a moment, and I thought he'd drifted off. Then he spoke, "I wanted to protect you, I guess. It seemed inconsequential. I mean, an old key could have belonged to anyone. The kids who shovel the paths, the paperboy, the people who lived there before. You had so much going on, you were this close to unraveling, and I just—"

I pressed my lips to the corner of his mouth. "Okay, it's cool. I get it."

"I wasn't thinking straight, I guess. I love you, and I worry about you, the weights that you carry. I meant to say something, but nothing more was ever said about that stupid key, so it kind of slid to the back of my mind and—"

This time I put my lips to his. "Thank you for being protective. I love that you look out for me." My thoughts went roundabout again, skipping in circles like kids around a maypole. "I'm just so confused. I mean, we broke up years ago. Has she been obsessing over me all this time? Why? I'm a nobody."

He pulled me closer until I was tight to his side. Then he ran his fingers over my jaw. "Benoit, you're as far from a nobody as anyone could ever be. You're an incredible young man standing on the cusp of greatness. I'm honored to be able to be beside you as you reach for the stars." He yawned then, a jaw-cracking thing, and his eyes began to flutter shut. Within seconds, he was snoring lightly. I had questions for him, about that key and what else he had kept from me, but as I lay there watching him sleep, I knew the answers would come eventually. Just not this morning. Eyes closing as his breathing soothed me, I dropped off quickly, my sleep deep and thankfully void of replays of the night, the crash, and the shining madness in Dom's eyes.

SIXTEEN

Benoit

THE NEXT GAME OF THE SERIES AGAINST THE OHIO STATE Otters, I sat out. It made me incredibly frustrated, but the team ophthalmologist had wanted to give my eye another week of rest. So, I rested my eye as I sat on the bench and watched my team crush the Otters. Sitting sucked. It gave me too much time to mull things over. My social media guy, and yes, I now had a guy because of the explosion that had taken place over Dom, the crash, the notes, the stalking, the cops putting cuffs on me, you name it, and the Internet had discussed it to death over the past seven days.

My social media guy, a young dude named Ulysses Shane, who had come recommended by Layton Foxx, was buffering as much as he could, spinning things to the best of his skills, but still, the furor raged on. Slurs and taunts from trolls were met with slurs and taunts from my defenders. It was, as Ryker had predicted, a shitstorm. And amid all of that, I had a boyfriend back in a cast, my family who'd been tracked down by the press, and reporters hounding me and the team wherever we went.

Maybe sitting out for a few more days was a good thing. It would get my head into the place it needed to be for the final game. Maybe Edmonton hadn't seen any of this mess. Maybe I could concentrate on classes. Maybe I could be in net the night we went up against the Montana U. Mountain Goats for the NCAA championship. Maybe it would all have blown over by Saturday when we played the Goats at the Lake Key Arena in Buffalo, New York. And maybe scallops would fly out of my pants to quote a famous cartoon crab.

IT HAD *NOT* BLOWN over by Saturday. But the credit for my focus and ability to slough off the media blitz was down to one person: Ethan. Well, maybe four people: Ethan, my mom, sister, and Dad. They'd flown out, on Ethan's tab, to see the game. That had meant so much to me that I cried when they arrived at the hotel in Buffalo. That weeping spell had purged all kinds of toxic crap. With my family, my team, and the man I loved crutching along at my side, I could do anything. The team ophthalmologist had cleared me for play, and we were now standing in the hallway outside our locker room, waiting to be announced to the over fourteen thousand people who had showed up. Due to the stories surrounding me, the game was actually being carried by a major sports network. Most NCAA hockey games weren't, so everyone was doubly nervous. Guess some good can come from bad stuff if you look hard enough.

I could taste the energy, excitement and adrenalin in that corridor. I'd already worked the ice, my mom making sure to bring me some fresh water from my home lake. There was nothing to do but wait and share in the routines. When our team was announced, we hit the ice, the fans rising to cheer us on just as the Montana U fans had. I went to my net, lowered my head, and listened to the anthem being sung, the madness of the past two weeks drifting away as the words to the song rose to the rafters. I took Dominque Wells and put her into a nook. The press and social media madness went into another nook. My father's health? Into a nook. My grades also into a nook. The fact that I'd been nominated for the Mike Richter Award and came second, which was damned amazing? Into a nook. Everything that wasn't this game went into a nook.

I worked my ice up, staring down at the beautiful blue under my skates, and felt my mind clearing, like by a gust of soft cold air over a pristine frozen Canadian lake. Serenity settled into my marrow, the upheaval of my life carried away. I inhaled the smell of ice and hockey, and I knew I was ready.

Good thing too, because the Goats had come to play. From the first puck drop, both teams were challenging each other. Wild momentum shifts caused by takeaways kept both us goalies on our toes. The defense on both sides were having issues with the faster skaters. For the Goats, it was a sophomore winger, Julian Peterson, who had moves that would rival Tennant Rowe in a few years. For us, it was Tennant Rowe's stepson, Ryker Madsen, who kept sneaking through gaps to take blistering shots on the Goats goalie. Ryker was going to light things *up* out in Phoenix in the fall. I prayed I'd be doing the same a little farther north.

The first period ended with both teams unable to score. The pep talk from Coach was loud, upbeat, and aimed at containing the breakaways and turnovers. With a defensive mindset, the Eagles went back out for a twenty-minute span of choking defensive play. The Goats coach must have filled their ears with the same speech. Shots on goal fell dramatically, and all the activity seemed to be in the neutral zone. I faced five shots in that period, the Goats goalie only four. The second intermission pep talk was similar to the first. Coach liked to see a tight D, and I wasn't about to complain. Twenty-two shots on goal in the first period versus five in the second? Yeah, I'd take that anytime. I was on top of my game as we went out for the last twenty minutes. All the distractions of life were tucked into my nooks. I'd have to send Stan Lyamin a thank-you note. Once I'd figured out what he'd meant, I'd been able to compartmentalize better.

The only glimmer of non-hockey life that snuck in was a short memory of the kiss Ethan had given me outside the locker room before the game. Right in front of my family, friends, and the press. Everyone knew we were a couple due to everything that had happened, so why hide it? That memory warmed me, and I eased back onto my heels in the crease, feeling the pipe resting on my back and knowing that the next twenty minutes were going to go my way. How could they not? I had Canadian ice under me, my family and friends cheering me on, and the man I loved sending me all the good vibes he could. The damn fool was probably waving his crutches in the air. He'd painted them Eagles brown and gold and was so damn proud of his work.

The shot on goal from the face-off woke me up. It was

an easy shot to stop, right to the chest, but it signaled a drastic change in the game. With two fat zeroes on the scoreboard, both teams were playing out and out balls to the wall. The fans were fully engaged, and the action began in my end with a mad flurry of shots. Several were quality attempts, and I was relieved to see the puck race down to the Goats' end for a spell. That was how it went, back and forth, end to end, until we had three minutes left and Julian Peterson broke free in the Goats' end and went coast-to-coast, his snapshot a blur that skipped across the rutted ice. I watched it racing toward me, calculated where it was headed, then began shifting to the left. The puck hit a groove in the ice and bounced in the opposite direction. I had a split second to throw my leg out. The tip of the skate was the only thing keeping that puck from sailing into my net.

The Eagles fans erupted and cheered my name. *Ben-Wah! Ben-Wah! Ben-Wah!* I was already past that save, my attention on the puck as Ryker picked it up in the corner, then passed it out of our zone. Some incredibly tight forechecking took place for about forty-seconds, and then it happened. A small mistake, a lack of communication, and the Goats coughed up the puck in their end. Ryker found the puck on his stick after a wobbly pass from Brandon Reynolds, who now played first line in Scott's place, at the blue line. He could have taken a wild slapshot and hoped for the best, but he didn't. He moved around a defender, made a hard cut to the net, and took his shot. The goalie was screened well, and the puck skimmed the edge of his blocker, rising high and clattering off the crossbar, then dropping down behind the goalie and rolling serenely over the line into the goal.

I leaped up and down in a lonely celebration dance as the rest of the line fell on Ryker in jubilation. They took their time getting back to the fist bump line. My heart was thundering. I glanced at the clock over center ice. One minute and fourteen-seconds left. I hunkered down and began whispering to the ice under me. Asking it to keep the pucks out of the net. I'd have dropped down and kissed that frozen water if I could have. But there was no time to smooch ice. The Goats pulled their goalie and the final seventy-four seconds was total bedlam in front of my net. Players were in front of me, in my crease, pushing and shoving and whacking at the puck as it was shot at me over and over. Ryker gave up his body once, taking a puck to the wrist that made his eyes water, but he refused to leave the ice. He was fine he said and shook his hand, his grimace worrisome.

The clock ran out during a mad rush of players. I heard the horn just as I fell over the puck, trapping it to the ice with my catcher and my blocker. Confetti guns loaded with brown and gold bits of paper went off, fans shouted, and my teammates piled onto my back. It was fucking fantastic! I lay there on the ice, laughing and crying, with twenty-some men rolling around on top of me. Ryker pulled me to my skates. We hugged. He was crying too.

The handshake line was tough for our opponents. But there can only be one winner, and that was us. We happily accepted that beautiful wood-and-glass trophy, holding it high over our heads and whooping it up. We rolled into the home locker room, riding a wave of sheer joy, our sweat-soaked jerseys still worn over our game-worn pads. No way were we seniors ready to take off our sweaters yet. This was our last game. We were prolonging the final hour.

Then we'd take them off forever. Talk about a bittersweet moment. The celebration went on for as long as we could make it; lots of nonalcoholic champagne was popped. Finally, when we could put it off no longer, the press was permitted in for a bit. I gave them a short sound bite, then went to the showers, leaving them with a practiced reply that Ulysses had sent me after the news of the win reached him. After the presser was over, the showers filled quickly. We were all eager to get to our friends and family and then celebrate with the Eagles fans who had come all the way to Buffalo.

The first person I saw when I left the locker room through the throng of people waiting in the family lounge was Ethan. He was balanced on his crutches, and the man was beaming. Face lit up like a lighthouse. My mom and dad were on either side of him, my sister off talking to some freshman forward who was leaning in a little too close for my liking. I pushed through the friends and family, skirting around the hugging parents and kissing girlfriend-boyfriends, to reach my folks. Dad kissed me on the cheek, his eyes red-rimmed from crying, his left hand firmly on his cane. Mom moved in next, weeping joyously and blabbering on about the proudest day of her life. Ethan smiled at me over her head as I held her close.

"Okay, okay, I've hogged you enough. Go give your man a hug." Mom patted my cheek, then nudged me to Ethan. I slid into him, my arms going around his waist, my lips finding his. We weren't the only LGBT couple sharing a smooch. Jacob and Ryker were wound around each other like creeping vines, Ryker's head resting on Jacob's shoulder, his grin wide. The man had a lot to smile about, Mr. Hobey Baker trophy winner. His future in Arizona was set in stone. I bet he even made the team right out of college. No minors for him. You could see the stardust settling on his shoulders. Maybe some of that sparkly stuff would fall on my head as well.

"You look lost," Ethan said when I pulled back to stare into those beautiful blue eyes of his. "Eye bothering you?"

"Nope, nothing is bothering right now. Right now, everything is about as perfect as it can be."

"Yeah? What about Charlie Wilkes over there chatting up Tamara?" He winked as he said it, knowing I took my role as big brother seriously.

"Well, *that's* not perfect, but everything else? Yeah. Everything else is damn fine right now."

SEVENTEEN

Ethan

I wasn't the kind of person who got star struck. Certainly not when faced with my best friend's little brother. Not only did I know Ten socially, a little anyway, but I'd played against him in a few games over the past couple of years. I'd even made the same top hundred best players list two years back. Of course he was third on the list, and I scraped in at ninety-eight. Still, it was the same list. Last time Boston had played the Railers, we'd had dinner with him and Jared, and it ws *Jared* was who I was star struck over. I hadn't managed more than two words with Jared Madsen over that meal, but that was mostly okay as I was down at the opposite end to him. He was one of the D-Men I'd respected the most, and I was gutted when he'd had to leave the game, always hoping that one day we'd, by magic, end up playing on the same team, and better than that, I could be his defense partner.

Me and Mads as a defensive pair? That would have been the coolest thing to happen in my entire hockey life. Only, of course, it never did happen, and it was really one of my only hockey regrets. Maybe it was that intense desire to play alongside him that had me hovering behind a tree right now, watching Mads, Ten, and Ryker huddled together and chatting.

"You have to go over there at some point, y'know."

I nearly jumped out of my skin and hobbled around to face Benoit, who was evidently more than a little amused at the fact that I was using the tree as protection.

"No. I don't," I said firmly. "I'll watch the entire graduation ceremony from here, safely behind my tree."

He chuckled and laced our fingers, and for a moment I thought he was going to kiss me, which was good because I needed all the kisses I could get. It was hot in the early Minnesota summer. My suit made me feel as if I was in a costume, and my leg ached like a bitch. Only there was no kissing. Instead, the little shit tugged me away from the tree, and given I was working on only one leg, I couldn't stop the motion, and there I was, in all my stupid ass glory with Jared *freaking* Madsen staring at me as if I was an idiot.

Which I was.

Then he strode toward me, his hand already extended, and I took it, and we shook hands firmly.

"Ethan, hey, shit luck with the leg," Mads began, Tennant and Ryker ambling over to join us.

"And your heart," I said, and then closed my mouth because... what the fuck? Who brought up heart issues. Not that Mads seemed upset. Instead, he shook his head ruefully.

"I always hoped that one day we'd end up on the same team," he announced and shrugged. "There was one chance, maybe five years ago. Boston was interested apparently, although that could have been my agent bullshitting me because there was no way they could have both of us, right? Imagine the salary cap hit on that." He elbowed Ten in the side and then Ryker. "Can't afford fancy overpriced centers like these two if a team spends all their money on defense."

I realized I was staring, and for an awkward moment, there was silence, and Mads stared at me with expectation.

"Who are you calling overpriced," Ten groused good-naturedly.

"I wish I *was* overpriced," Ryker added.

Then it all spilled out from me as I ignored both Ten and Ryker. "I feel exactly the same. You're one of the only D-men I regret never having skated with." There, I'd said it and felt a hundred times better.

Mads gestured at my leg. "Get that fixed, and we'll set up a game."

We chatted for a while then until it was time for Benoit, Ryker, and Scott to head off for the ceremony. Benoit looked particularly fine today, in a dark suit, his robes graceful around him, and he was smiling. He hadn't stopped smiling since the last day when he'd handed in his thesis and taken his final exams, and he was done with college. He'd be heading to training camp soon, had passed with flying colors, and was now on a two-way contract with Edmonton. With the fact that the team was down a goalie maybe, *just maybe*, he'd be back up for the NHL team instead of the minors. Who knew?

"This is it," he murmured, and he hugged his family close.

His dad was obviously tired, but he was on a new drug regime, and it seemed to be helping with his sarcoidosis.

Of course, Benoit didn't know it was me funding the program, and I'm not sure I'd tell him until that perfect moment when I knew his pride wouldn't get in the way. I was doing it for his dad, and the secret was his and mine to keep. Although given the way Benoit's mom kept looking at me as if she was going to burst into tears, then clung to me in the tightest mom-hug ever, it might not stay a secret for long.

Then it was my turn. I tugged him close to me, held him tight.

"I'm so proud of you, Benoit. So proud of everything you've done, and of what I know you're going to do." He pressed a kiss to my hand, smiled at us all, then jogged to catch up with Scott, falling into pace next to him as they headed for their chairs.

I kept it together for the ceremony, my chest near bursting with pride when the dean called his name. He grinned at the audience, right at where I was sitting with his family, Hayne, and a super emotional Jacob, then let out a whoop and punched the air. He and Scott did this weird-ass dance. Then Ryker joined in, and the three of them ended up in the crowd of undergrads taking photos, shouting, laughing, celebrating everything that was utterly perfect in this moment in their lives.

"You know, I think I might want to do this college thing," Mads said as we watched. "I missed out."

"Me too, but we still had one hell of a ride without it."

We exchanged thoughtful smiles, both of us onto the next steps in our life. For me, the next big thing was deciding on a career path. I knew *where* I was going, and that was anywhere Benoit went, but doing what, I didn't know. I'd put out feelers with several contacts in sports representation, including signaling interest in a couple of positions with Edmonton. One of them in particular, as the video coach, was something I was really interested in, only I had one worry I couldn't shake. Maybe it wouldn't be right with Benoit playing there. What if they didn't like that? Not every team management was as enlightened as the Railers.

"Penny for them," Benoit said at my side.

"Nah, I'd want at least a dollar," I said.

"Not sure I can afford a whole dollar," Ben teased. "You ready to go?"

We joined everyone else and headed for The Aviary, their coffee place turned into a space for celebration today. The door was wide open, students and parents spilling out onto the grass outside, sprawled on the ground with plates of food and plastic glasses of something fizzy. We grabbed food, pulled one of the tables from inside, collected chairs, and all sat around in a big informal circle.

The only dark spot was when Charlie Wilkes joined us by dragging over a chair and sitting next to a beaming Tamara.

"I'm gonna kill him," Benoit muttered under his breath so only I could hear.

I loved his big brother routine, the one where he was going to hurt anyone who went anywhere near his sister. In fact, I loved everything about him from his nose to his toes and everything in between.

"I love you," I blurted, and he shot me a grin.

"So you'll help me find somewhere to bury Charlie?" He seemed pathetically hopeful.

"No, but I'll wait for you to get out of prison."

He shook his head. "You're not the man I thought you were."

This kind of back and forth, a lighter Benoit, was lovely to see. After the whole Dom situation, things had been dark for a while. She was receiving psychiatric care, and I hoped she received all the help she needed. I hadn't exactly forgiven what she did, but Benoit seemed to have gotten to a good place right now, and I wasn't going to rock the boat. I just wanted to have this, and him, for the rest of my life.

"Benoit?" I asked cautiously, the words I really wanted to say on the tip of my tongue.

"Yeah?"

I never got the chance to vocalize the thoughts I had when Ryker crouched in front of us and glanced up at me. "Coach Girard, do you think we could talk? If you have a minute?"

"You can call me Ethan now, you know."

He shook his head, with his stubborn-Ryker expression very obvious. "You'll always be Coach Girard to me."

"Benoit? You should follow Ryker's example," I said with a laugh.

Benoit shook his head. "If you think I'm calling you Coach Girard for the rest of our lives, you're mistaken."

"Well, damn," I joked and then stood up, leaning on my cane. "Of course we can talk."

Ryker walked away from the group, and I followed until we reached a stand of trees. I seemed to be spending a lot of time in and around trees today.

"What's up?" I asked, although I had a good idea of what he wanted to ask me. Benoit had already explained that Ryker was growing more messed up about joining the

Raptors training camp in fifteen weeks. I guess he couldn't really unload on his dad and Ten, not after what had happened to Ten. I bet Mads was worried about his son playing with the man who'd nearly killed Ten.

Ryker cleared his throat. "So, Jacob said I should talk to someone who isn't Dad or Ten. I'd just like your take on things. The Raptors... I could turn them down, right? I mean, there have been drafted players who refuse to play for the team that drafted them if the franchise is struggling, like Zach Hyman did in 2010."

"Yeah, that can happen, but the team could make things really bad for you, lock you up in contracts for the longest time, alter future events on both sides of the table. You could lose a year, and your career might never recover."

Ryker kicked at a blade of grass, disgust in every line of him. "Everyone knows that the Raptor's strategy right now is to aim low and secure a high draft pick. I don't want that. I want a team that plays to win every damn time they hit the ice."

He was right. It was easy to see that the Raptors had pushed out some crappy results last year, finishing fourth from the bottom of the table, and it could be said they were doing this deliberately. So much so that they might do the same thing again this next season. I understood Ryker's reluctance completely.

"You're not a quitter, Ryker," I reassured him.

He frowned. "But what if the rest of the team are?"

I wished I had wisdom to give him, words that sounded clever and meant something, but I had none, and in the end, I went with a blunt assessment of the situation.

"Even if you hate it, you keep your head down, you

work hard, and you shine the brightest you can among the crap you've landed in. The Raptors are in a bad place, yeah, but every team has had its bad times. You need to get in there and make a difference from the inside out."

He looked so hopeful for a moment. "You think I could change things?"

"I don't see why not." I clapped a hand on his shoulder. "Hockey is like a game of chess. Stay patient, keep thinking, and you'll make it out the other side."

"Chess with hip checks," Ryker pointed out, and I tightened my grip on him briefly.

"Yeah, imagine it as chess with hip checks if that makes it better."

Benoit hovered at a distance, and Ryker waved him over, exchanged fist bumps before leaving, and then it was just Benoit, me, and the big old tree.

"You fixed everything?" he said and handed me his drink.

I sipped the fizz and then nodded. "Clearly, I am a god to all young hockey players," I deadpanned. "I know all, see all, and—"

He stopped me with a kiss, and the fizz slopped over the edge and down my shirt. I didn't care. I wanted all of his kisses, all the time.

"You should marry me," I announced when we parted to take a breath, and his eyes widened. God, I hadn't meant to drop that on him so dramatically. "Shit. Listen to me. I have a job offer from Edmonton, okay, but I worry they'll do that whole thing about not dating a teammate, but we wouldn't be dating; we'd be married. Like permanently together." He seemed shocked and had gone very quiet. "Benoit? Say something? Fuck, it's too soon, right? I've messed this up. I should have waited for—"

Yet again, he stopped me from talking with a kiss, and as usual, I let him. Anything not to hear his reasons why what I'd asked was a bad idea. But when we separated, he was grinning at me.

"Yes," he said with conviction and no hesitation at all

"Really?"

"Hell, yes."

"There's something you should know first." I had to be honest about the money I'd used for his dad, and it had to be now that I told him.

He sighed dramatically. "Okay, but is this about your snoring because I already know that. Or is it that you're funding the medication for my dad?" He tilted his head, and I was tongue-tied.

"You... how... who...?"

He tapped my nose. "You think my mom could keep that secret? I love you for doing it, but I will be paying every cent back when I'm earning my millions."

"You can put the money in a trust fund for the kids." *What? What did I just say?*

His mouth fell open. "Kids?" he squeaked, then cleared his throat.

"Maybe," I offered cautiously and waited for Benoit to run away screaming.

"Okay then, I can do that. Marry you, be a professional NHL goalie, have a big house with a yard in Edmonton, get two dogs, then add kids to the mix."

"Two dogs? What if I'm a cat man?"

He faked horror and punched my arm. "It's like I don't even know you." Then he sobered and cradled my face.

"We're getting married." He sounded so blown away, as if me asking him had rocked his world, and I hoped it had because the thought of being together forever was my only focus. "I love you."

"I love you, Benoit, but there's one thing we need to clear up."

"What?"

"I don't freaking snore."

Epilogue

BENOIT

THE SUN CREEPING THROUGH OUR BEDROOM WINDOW WOKE me. I rolled to my left, to hide my face from the bright rays, but couldn't get to my other side, due to a warm body taking up all the room. Grunting a bit, I shimmied around until I could stare at Ethan sleeping. His face was soft in repose, his lips parted, his arm flung over the pillow. He was breathtaking with the soft glow of morning on his whiskery face. The need to touch him was overpowering, so I ran a hand over his back, enjoying the swells and valleys. From his deltoids to his obliques to his firm glutes, the man was hard and toned, a masculine creation of beauty who belonged in one of Hayne's paintings. The thought of Hayne reminded me of FaceTime Friday, the one day of the week we all took thirty minutes—or longer —to touch base.

Now that Ryker, Scott, and I had graduated and had gone our separate ways, it was important to all of us to maintain contact. They were my best friends, my teammates… well, not anymore. As of tomorrow's opening day of training camp, I'd be wearing the orange Edmonton home jersey. How long I stayed in that jersey all depended on if I made the main team. Not everyone who was drafted did. Some tried out and were sent to the feeder teams. I felt confident about my chances. Scott and I were sure about Ryker's. He was going to set the hockey world on fire.

I leaned over Ethan, pressed a kiss to his spine, inhaled his scent, and then slid from the bed and pulled on some lounge pants. My routine since moving to Edmonton with Ethan three weeks ago didn't vary. Wake up, look down on the city as I did a moment of thanks, yoga for thirty, shower, gym, ice time, home to Ethan. Routine was critically important. At least for my goalie mind, it was. I padded to the sliding doors and pulled them open, stepping out onto the balcony with a view of Ellerslie Road. Our apartment complex was in a high-class community close to Blackburn Creek Park and only twenty minutes from the arena. We'd chosen a two-bedroom unit already furnished, my fiancé stating he was a decorating slob who couldn't care less if the throw pillows coordinated with the drapes. I really had no time to devote to kitting out a place, so fully furnished it was.

Edmonton was already awake and moving at seven in the morning. I drank in the city, enjoying the blue skies and cool fifty-degree air on my bare chest. Canada. No matter where I went in my homeland, I could always feel the sense of home.

My skin pimpled up when a light breeze tickled the sides of the blue-and-white building. We were only four floors up. That was as high as all the elite buildings in this small grouping went. Sneaking back inside, I went to the guest room, leaving Ethan snoozing, and unrolled my mat.

I took several minutes to center, legs folded into a lotus, and then began my morning sun salutation. I'd let my mind wander, and it landed on Dom. She'd been shipped back to Canada for her trial. Her sentence had been light as I had advocated for her to be placed into a mental health facility instead of serving time in prison. She'd never had a good home life and had no one on her side, her parents having long ago slid into bottles of vodka. It had been tough to turn the other cheek, and every time I saw Ethan's slight limp, I questioned the advice my folks and Ethan had given me. But what was done was done. She was getting help for her mental health issues, and I'd attempted to get past it. Mostly. Unless it was dark and Ethan was driving, or a pink envelope appeared in our mailbox. Then I'd get a flashback, but other than that, I was working my way through it. We all were. It was the only thing to do. Move forward or get mired down in the past.

When I was done, I thanked the universe for all the blessings in my life. Then I raced to the kitchen, fired up the Keurig, fixed myself a twisted cherry protein shake and a bowl of fruit and yogurt, and dropped down at the island —where we ate all of our meals—and opened Ethan's laptop.

Ryker, who was in the same time zone as I was and probably rolling out for his day, quickly accepted the request to FaceTime. Scott, who was an hour ahead of us, but never seemed to be in any hurry to get up, took longer to answer the call. When he did, the loser was still in bed, his hair a ratty mess.

"Dude, you have pink paint on your face," Ryker immediately pointed out. The lump behind him in bed giggled. Ryker rolled his eyes. I almost inhaled a grape whole when Ethan slid up behind me, arms going around my midsection, his warm lips falling to my shoulder.

"Morning," he murmured against my skin. "Hey, guys," he said to Ryker and Scott, his voice still thick with sleep. After a quick hug, he grabbed a cup of coffee, gave me a wink, and went off to read the morning paper out on the balcony. I hoped he'd pulled on some clothes before he plunked his ass into one of our white patio chairs.

"Okay, I am totally filing the past two minutes under hashtag envious," Ryker grumbled, then shoved his hands through his still damp curls.

"Sorry," Scott and I both mumbled.

Ryker had left Jacob behind on the farm a week ago to settle into his new place in Tucson. I felt really bad for them having to be that far apart. How they'd juggle their relationship with that great of a distance was beyond me. I worried for the two of them but kept my concerns to myself.

"No, don't be sorry. I'm being petty. I just…" He blew a strand of hair from his face. "This is the dream, am I right?"

"Yeah, man," I replied as Scott yawned and sat up slowly, his eyes flickering from Hayne at his side, then back to us. "I mean, for me it is."

"My dream is right here." Scott patted the energetic mound of artist hiding under the covers next to him. Another short burst of giggles could be heard. "Well, this and working with the kids at the rink. We're kicking off our special needs skates tomorrow. Did I mention that?"

"Yeah, man, that's super cool," Ryker said, lifting his phone from the counter and crossing to his tiny and kind of bare living room. His place was nice. All shades of tan and brown and white, very desert motif, which fit his locale well. "I hope we can set up some programs out here like that. Community things. This team tanks at that. Well, they tank at mostly everything but…" He shrugged.

"You'll get them moving in the right direction," I said, forking up a chunk of pineapple, then dipping it into the mound of vanilla yogurt. Damn, this fruit was good. Ethan did groceries like a pro, filling the fridge with good food suited for an athlete.

"Totally," Scott piped up, rolling his neck in a circle. "I'm thinking of going for my master's. Maybe in special education. Want to see how things go with the Special Skates, but I'm really feeling this project."

"That would be epic," Ryker said. I nodded. As long as Scott was happy and not abusing, I was all for whatever career choice fulfilled him. With Hayne at his side, I was sure he'd have a loving and happy life. "Oh wow, dudes…"

I chewed, swallowed, and waited for Ryker to speak.

"Okay, wow, so I'm kind of reading the team group chat. Looks like the talk about bringing in Rowen Carmichael as the new head coach will be announced today. Shit, that's kind of awesome! He's coached at UWO for five years and led the Mustangs to two U sports championships. Cool. So, that's good news. I like this trend of picking up college coaches for the pros. They know how to guide young players."

"That is cool!" I gushed. "I seriously looked into UWO as a top three contender when I was picking colleges. I bet you'll do great under Rowen Carmichael. Everything I read about him when I was scoping out the team was positive."

"Yeah, maybe they're seriously going to try to clean up this fucking team. First thing they need to do is trade asshole Lankinen to the Siberian Front league. I'm going to have to go in there in two days and look at his fucking face."

Scott and I both sat silently. What could we say? Yeah, Ryker was going to have to share a locker room with the man who'd nearly ended Tennant Rowe's career. I did not envy Ryker anything.

"Just show them you're above the shit. Aarni will hang himself if you give him enough rope," I finally said. Scott bobbed his head.

"Yeah, I know. I'm just… gah. Whatever. I'm a Raptor, and I'm going to go in there and give them one hundred percent. We Madsens play hard, and we play to win."

Scott and I cheered. The talk then shifted to less intense shit like food, movies, and life far away from the dry, hot winds that blew around the Santa Catalina Arena. After we hashed out the latest YouTube controversy, we all had to cut off the call and tend to life things. Scott to work at the rink, Ryker and I prepping for our first ever professional training camps. With a vow to talk next Friday and well wishes, I closed the laptop, grabbed my fruit cup, and went in search of my man.

He was on the patio, in a hoodie and matching jogging pants, his feet in thick slippers, reading the paper and drinking his coffee.

"You look cold," I said as I stepped out to join him.

He gave me a fast once-over. "I *am* cold. I'm old. My

blood flow isn't good anymore. Get me a hot water bottle and a handful of stool softeners, sonny."

"Poor old man." I closed the door, placed my breakfast on the white metal table our two chairs sat by, and straddled his lap, dropping myself to his thighs, then pressing against him, my hands sliding up into his tousled hair. "Let me warm you up. I've got plenty of blood racing through my young veins." I rolled my hips so he could feel my lengthening dick on his stomach. "See?"

"Ah, youth." He sighed, dropping his newspaper to the cement so that he could cradle my ass as I tongued his throat. "You and the boys get things talked out for the week?"

"Mm, yeah, Scott's thinking of maybe more school. Special education."

"Oh? Good on him."

"Ryker is trying to be upbeat, but he misses Jacob, and the Raptors are… well, the Raptors."

"Poor guy," he replied, giving my ass cheeks a firm squeeze. I nibbled along the shell of his ear, my half-hard dick fully erect now.

"Yeah, they got a new coach coming in, rumors. Rowen Carmichael. Man, you taste good. Getting warm yet, gramps?"

"Getting there. Keep whispering dirty hockey nothings in my ear while you hump my dick, and I'll be all kinds of toasty warm."

"We could go back to bed. I don't have to be at the gym until nine, and your new job as video coach…"

"Begins today." He sighed sadly. "I want to be there early to meet with the rest of the coaching staff before you chuckleheads arrive tomorrow. So, unfortunately, your young blood will have to cool off until tonight."

I moaned in the most morose way I could. Yeah, sure, we'd just made love last night, but that was, like, nine hours ago…

"I'm not sure I like this adulting shit," I complained as I burrowed my nose into his thick hair.

"You missing Owatonna already?"

I sat back after a moment to seriously consider his question. He waited patiently, as he always did for me to arrive at the place I needed to be. That was just one of the many things I loved about him: his patience.

"Yeah, I do miss it. I mean, your college years are special. It's where you find out who you are, right?" He shrugged, and I felt bad. "You could do some online courses. You and Jared. You'd ace it. Smart, sexy man like you."

"Mm, well, I *did* ask you to marry me, so I guess I am pretty fucking brilliant."

Yep, he was. And I was brilliant to say yes.

THE END

Coming next in the Owatonna U Hockey series

Christmas Lights (Owatonna U, 4)

Christmas Lights

Under the Christmas lights strung outside a snowy Minnesota cabin, Ryker and Jacob face a future where nothing will be the same again.

Fortunate timing means that Ryker and Jacob can spend a few days together over Christmas in a cabin on the family farm. What's better is that Scott and Ben are coming as well, with Hayne and Ethan in tow. Ryker can't imagine a better way to spend time with the man he loves, and the friends he misses, and somehow he knows that this Christmas will be the best one ever. Hockey on a frozen pond, kisses under Christmas lights, and sharing time with Jacob are the best gifts he could ever receive.

Long distance relationships are brutal, Jacob can attest to that fact. So, when Ryker gets a few days off over the Raptors' Christmas break, the hard-working Minnesota farmer is beyond thrilled. When they find out that their buddies from Owatonna U. are making the trip as well, the holidays are looking to be just about perfect. Jacob has a question for Ryker burning in his heart, and he isn't asking for much—just a few fun-filled days with old friends and a yes from the man of his dreams.

Christmas Lights

Harrisburg Railers

Owatonna U Hockey

Arizona Raptors

Boston Rebels

LA Storm

Chesterford Coyotes - Young Adult

Harrisburg Railers

When hockey wunderkind Tennant Rowe meets his new coach, he knows he's in trouble. Jared Madsen is nine years older than Tennant, impossibly attractive, and — worst of all — his brother's off-limits best friend. Is their chemistry worth the risk?

Changing Lines (Railers 1)

Can Tennant show Jared that age is just a number, and that love is all that matters?

The Rowe Brothers are famous hockey hotshots, but as the youngest of the trio, Tennant has always had to play against his brothers' reputations. To get out of their shadows, and against their advice, he accepts a trade to the Harrisburg Railers, where he runs into Jared Madsen. Mads is an old family friend and his brother's one-time teammate. Mads is Tennant's new coach. And Mads is the sexiest thing he's ever laid eyes on.

Jared Madsen's hockey career was cut short by a fault in his heart, but coaching keeps him close to the game. When Ten is traded to the team, his carefully organized world is thrown into chaos. Nine years his junior and his best friend's brother, he knows Ten is strictly off-limits, but as soon as he sees Ten's moves, on and off the ice, he knows that his heart could get him into trouble again.

Changing Lines

Harrisburg Railers (Hockey Romance)

1. Changing Lines
2. First Season
3. Deep Edge
4. Poke Check
5. Last Defense
6. Goal Line
7. Neutral Zone
8. Hat Trick
9. Save The Date
10. Baby Makes Three
11. Rivals
12. Perfect Gifts
13. Family First

Railers Volume 1 | Railers Volume 2 | Railers Volume 3 | Railers Volume 4

Coast to Coast (Arizona Raptors 1)

Coast To Coast

When opposites attract, this bottom-of-the-league team will never be the same again.

A stipulation in his father's will forces Mark back into the arms of a family that disowned him and leaves him one-third owner of a hockey team facing financial ruin. He doesn't even watch hockey, let alone like it, and wants nothing more than to head back to New York. Then there's the new coach, a stubborn, opinionated, irritating man with superiority issues and questionable music taste. Butting heads with Rowen becomes the new normal, but it comes with passionate debate and an all-consuming lust.

Challenged to rebuild one of the worst teams in the league into a future cup contender, Rowen can't pass up the opportunity. Never in his twenty years of hockey has he ever seen a team managed so badly or coached players overflowing with resentment and bigotry. Yet there's something about this team and this city that compels him to roll up his sleeves and start dismantling. If only Mark, one of three siblings who now own the Raptors, wasn't so damned rock-headed yet so damned appealing his job might be easier. It doesn't look like either is willing to give in, but one night in a dark, desert hotel changes everything.

Coast To Coast

Arizona Raptors (Hockey Romance)

1. Coast To Coast
2. Across the Pond
3. Shadow and Light
4. Sugar and Ice
5. School and Rock

Boston Rebels

Top Shelf (Boston Rebels 1)

Top Shelf

Acting on the attraction to his best friend's brother has always been off the table for Xander until a passionate hookup with Mason at a beach resort begins a love affair that burns long after summer ends.

Mason specializes in assisting same-sex couples on their journey to becoming parents and fighting every rule that blocks his way in the stuck-in-the-past agency that hired him. Living in his brother's pool house is rent-free, and every cent he earns he saves for his dream—that one day he'd have his own company helping others. The downside is that he has to see his annoying brother every day, the upside is that his brother's teammates from the Boston Rebels make regular visits. The eye candy that passes Mason's window is almost enough to make him consider dating a hockey player, but not just any player though. Ever since Xander —his brother's childhood friend—came out as gay at a press conference, Mason's puppy love has turned into a burning attraction he can no longer ignore.

Hockey has been one of Xander's main focuses since he was old enough to balance on skates. Well, hockey and Mason Kingsley, but Mason was always unattainable. Now that he's about to see thirty candles on his birthday cake and is no longer hiding the fact he's gay, he's ready to find a soul mate to make his life complete. A summer vacation is just what he needs to have time to think, but when the Boston Rebels arriving in paradise with Mason in tow, thinking is the last thing he needs. One torrid night under a balmy moon and rules about not messing with his best friend's brother vanish on a warm, tropical breeze.

Summer romances don't generally last past Labor Day, but with the new season about to begin Xander and Mason are going to have to face the world and decide if their love is real enough to withstand everything.

Top Shelf

Boston Rebels

Lost In Boston (Free Prequel Novella)

1. Top Shelf
2. Back Check

3. Snowed
4. Royal Lines
5. Blade
6. Rental

LA Storm

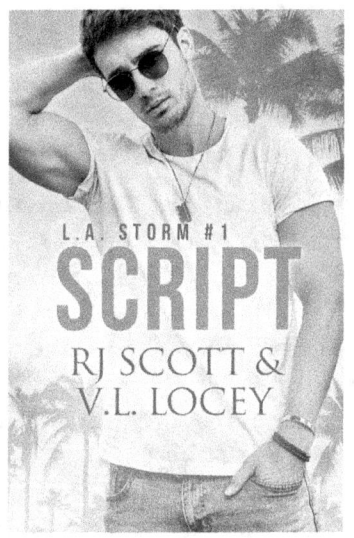

Script (LA Storm, 1)

Script

Hollywood A-lister Finn might be Canadian, but he needs Cameron to show him how to hockey.

Actor Finn Kerrigan is at a crossroads. After growing up a soap star, then starring in a hugely successful trilogy of action movies, he's finally given the chance to read a heartfelt and passionate script that could change his life forever. The role would be enough for people to see him as a serious actor, and maybe even win him an award or two (and no, a golden raspberry award for his action movies doesn't count). Once established as a serious actor he's sure he can come out of the closet and finally live his truth. When he lies to get the part of a hockey player on a struggling team, he suddenly has nowhere to hide. He might be Canadian, but the last time he skated he was ten, and no, he doesn't have hockey in his blood. With only a month until filming starts, he about to be exposed, but partnered with a player who's supposed to be giving him tips, he doesn't realize how many of his secrets will come to light. Falling in lust, one heated kiss at a time, is inevitable, but giving Cameron up at the end of the shoot could break his heart.

Cameron Chavkin is the face of the LA Storm. And the body, and the hair, and the smile. He's at the prime of his career, men and women want to be with him, and he's skating better than he ever has before. His house sits next to a famous rock star's mansion, his garage is filled with expensive cars, and he's even been asked to mentor a once-famous actor in a new hockey movie. Life is pretty sweet. Until the bad boy of hockey meets Finn, a man on the edge with more secrets than Cameron has endorsements. Knowing better than to get involved, Cameron is swept up despite himself, and when it's time to say goodbye to the Storm's most eligible bachelor is finding it hard to follow the script.

Script

LA Storm

1. Script
2. Second
3. Shield
4. Spiral

Off The Ice (Chesterford Coyotes, 1)

Off The Ice

A coming-of-age love story with high school, hockey rivalry, friendship, family, and coming out.

Soren's life changes in an instant when he and his younger brother are adopted by hockey royalty. Making sense of his new life is hard enough, but when he's enrolled in a private school it means facing a whole new set of problems. Navigating friendship, family, and hockey is one thing, but being attracted to the boy who vexes him is a whole new thing.

Felix has a reputation to protect. He's the kid who seems to have everything but looks can be deceiving. Spinning lies about his perfect life, he's created a fantasy world that even he has started to believe. Only, it's not long before everything crumbles, all of his pretty lies are revealed, and only his closest rival sees through his pain and stands by him.

Fighting is easy, friendship is hard, but love is everything.

Off The Ice

Chesterford Coyotes

1. Off The Ice
2. On Thin Ice
3. *Dance on Ice*

Also By RJ Scott

For a full list of ebooks and links please scan the code above or
visit rjscott.co.uk/rjbooks

Meet RJ Scott

RJ discovered romance in books at a very young age and realized that if there wasn't romance on the page, she could create it in her head. With over one hundred and fifty books published, she is a full time author of gay romance.

She lives and works out of her home in the beautiful English countryside, spends her spare time reading, watching films, and enjoying time with her family.

The last time she had a week's break from writing she didn't like it one little bit and has yet to meet a box of chocolates she couldn't defeat.

www.rjscott.co.uk | rj@rjscott.co.uk

NEWSLETTER - rjscott.co.uk/rjnews

facebook.com/author.rjscott

x.com/Rjscott_author

instagram.com/rjscott_author

amazon.com/author/rj-scott

bookbub.com/authors/rj-scott

goodreads.com/rjscott

pinterest.com/rjscottauthor

Also By VL Locey

For a full list of ebooks and links please scan the code above or visit vllocey.com/stories-from-vl-locey

Meet V.L. Locey

V.L. Locey loves worn jeans, yoga, belly laughs, walking, reading and writing lusty tales, Greek mythology, the New York Rangers, comic books, and coffee.

(Not necessarily in that order.)

She shares her life with her husband, her daughter, one dog, two cats, a flock of assorted domestic fowl, and two Jersey steers.

When not writing spicy romances, she enjoys spending her day with her menagerie in the rolling hills of Pennsylvania with a cup of fresh java in hand.

vllocey.com
vicki@vllocey.com

Newsletter - vllocey.com/newsletter

facebook.com/V.L.Locey

x.com/vllocey

instagram.com/vl_locey

bookbub.com/authors/v-l-locey

goodreads.com/vllocey

pinterest.com/vllocey